MARIE FERRARELLA

This *USA TODAY* bestselling and RITA® Award-winning author has written over 175 books for Silhouette Books, some under the name Marie Nicole. Her romances are beloved by fans worldwide. Check out her website at www.marieferrarella.com

In memory of my mother and father, who took the English language to places it had never been before.

Chapter 1

Natalya Pulaski closed the outer door to her third-floor office and flipped the lock. A heartfelt, weary sigh escaped her lips.

Well, that was the last of them.

Barring an emergency, she qualified, rubbing the raw spot on the side of her neck the last patient had awarded her when he made a sudden grab for the pendant that had dangled so temptingly before him. She had been leaning forward to check on the condition of the little boy's ears at the time. The chain had bitten into her skin before she and Julian's mother had managed to untangle the boy's forceful little fingers from the death grip he had on her necklace.

Julian's strength was head and shoulders above his age group, Natalya thought as she retreated to her inner office, turning lights off as she went. No doubt about it, Mr. and Mrs. Sands had a pro wrestler in their future.

And she, Natalya silently promised herself, had a hot bath in her immediate future. Visions of soaking in a tub amid fragrant bubbles had practically been all that had kept her going the last two hours of what felt like a marathon day.

It *had* been a marathon day, she reminded herself.

It had begun at six with a hysterical phone

call from a first-time mother. Marion Walters thought that everything was an emergency when it came to her month-old baby. It had taken Natalya almost ten minutes to ascertain that the "horrible skin condition" was actually a bad case of diaper rash. Even in the silence that engulfed her now, Natalya could still hear a mixture of Marion's wails accompanied by Justin's lusty crying.

By the time she'd managed to calm the woman down, Natalya found herself wide-awake. With two hours to go before her actual day began, she'd decided she might as well get a jump on things and possibly finish early for a change.

Natalya smiled to herself. After all this time, she was still an optimist. The best laid plans of mice and men and newly minted pediatricians often went astray. In her case, it was because Vicki, her nurse/receptionist, had overbooked her once again. She was beginning to think that Vicki had trouble remembering how many minutes were in an hour.

Determined to see all of her patients in a timely fashion, Natalya found herself without so much as two minutes to rub together.

Her overcrowded day had left her struggling with a fairly uncommon bout of irritability. Although, in her own defense, trying to make an accurate diagnosis could be absolutely ex-asperating when over half her patients couldn't answer her question "where does it hurt?"

Natalya shed her lab coat and hung it on the hook behind her door. That was probably the most frustrating part of being a pediatrician, she thought—the difficulty in communicating. Of course, sometimes it was still easier communi-cating with her young patients than it was talking with their parents. The latter were divided into two categories: those who were working parents who had taken time off to bring their child in and needed to get back to the rat race and those who were stay-at-home parents whose days were filled with wall-to-wall complaining. Both had one thing in common. They wanted their children cured yesterday.

She supposed she couldn't blame them, Natalya mused, crossing to her desk. If she had kids and they were ill, she'd want them well again at the speed of light.

Not that that scenario was ever going to happen, she thought ruefully. The dire sentence she'd had pronounced to her at the age of eighteen was still as true now as it had been then. Because of a severe case of endometriosis, the joy of experiencing motherhood firsthand had been taken away from her. She was never going to be able to feel life moving inside her. Never going to push a tiny being out into the world after chewing off half her lower lip to keep from screaming.

What had happened at eighteen had shaped the rest of her life. When she'd entered medical school, there had never been a question as to what path she would take once the diploma was in her hand. If she couldn't have a baby of her own, at least she could still hold them, help them, nurture them, which was why she'd become a pediatrician. And she kept very busy, so that the inherent loneliness of her life sentence never had a chance to infiltrate her soul for long.

But this pace did have its draining moments.

Natalya closed her eyes and leaned back in her chair for just a moment. She knew she should be making a hasty retreat before someone called the office with yet another emergency, but she just couldn't make herself get up. Besides, escape was never a sure thing, not where she was concerned. The answering service had her number. As did a few of the more worried patients, like Mrs. Sands. And there was no question that, if someone called, she would go.

Natalya shifted in her seat and her shoulders announced their displeasure. God, she hoped the tub was free. Although there were two bathrooms in the apartment, only one had a tub.

That was what she got for sharing a place with two of her sisters. Not that Sasha was going to be there much longer. Now that sexy-as-all-hell Detective Anthony Santini had finally proposed to her older sister, Natalya was certain they'd be getting married soon. That left her and Kady—until Tatania joined them come June.

Little Tania, a doctor. *Wow.* And Marja wasn't far behind.

Natalya smiled to herself. She had no right to be weary. Her parents, now *they* had a right to be weary. There were times she wondered how her parents had done it. Granted, she and Sasha helped out with any spare money they earned, but putting five daughters through medical school even took a toll on families who were far better off then hers. Still, it was her parents' dream—admittedly her mother's more than her father's—to have all of their children become doctors.

That—she'd heard more than once—was the reason why they had left their native Poland in the first place: to give the family they were planning all the advantages they never had. All the advantages that a country like the

United States could give. And no amount of sacrifices for either of them had been too much to achieve this goal.

Natalya suddenly realized that her eyes had closed.

"If you don't move in the next couple of minutes, Nat, you're going to fall asleep right here," she muttered under her breath.

Hands gripping the armrests on her office chair, she was about to propel herself into a standing position when she heard the beginning notes of "I've Got Plenty of Nothing" break through the silence.

Resigned, Natalya removed her hands from the armrests and fished out her cell phone from her skirt pocket. So much for making an escape.

Taking a deep breath, she pulled herself together and looked down at the LED screen on her phone. The name that flashed across it told her that her caller wasn't the parents of one of her patients.

It was Clancy.

She stifled a groan. "I'm too tired, Clancy," she protested to the ringing phone.

She and Clancy Donovan had been best friends since the time she'd come to his defense in the school cafeteria when three bullies had ganged up on him. Ever for the underdog, she'd shamed the bullies into backing off. Even at ten, she'd always known what to say or do in any given situation.

The cell phone rang again. She continued to look at it, working her lower lip between her teeth.

She'd forgotten. Forgotten that she'd promised Clancy to go with him to that new show that was opening at the art gallery tonight. Mrs. Levinson and her overactive twins, in for their child care checkups, had knocked that right out of her memory bank. It was around that time that she'd begun to fantasize about soaking in a hot tub until the end of time.

For a second, Natalya debated not answering the phone. After all, there were times when she did shut off her cell phone because it interfered with some of the equipment at the hospital.

But that would be just the coward's way out. She didn't believe in deception. And Clancy would be crushed if he ever found out that she'd deliberately ignored him.

Bracing herself—because Clancy was not the type to give up once he had set his mind to something—she flipped open the phone and placed it against her ear.

"Hi, Clancy. Look, I know I said I was going to go with you to that gallery opening tonight, but I am just wiped out." She knew how much he hated going anywhere alone so she quickly added, "I could see if Kady's doing anything."

Her younger sister, Leokadia, thought that Clancy was a little strange, but, like her, she regarded him as a lost soul. And Kady had come to appreciate the fact that Clancy was steadfast. He took the title of friend seriously and did whatever was required of him to maintain that position. Despite all his quirks, loyalty was never a question.

Taking a breath, Natalya waited for a response on the other end but there was none.

Okay, so he was hurt. It wasn't as if this was the first time. She could deal with that. "Clancy, I've had one of those days they write sitcoms around. I didn't even have time for lunch today."

There was still no response on the other end. She could just see him feeling rejected. Guilt began to prick at the edges of her conscience like tiny nettles in a field of overgrown weeds.

Maybe this was a really big deal for him. She supposed she could muster up some strength. After all, she'd managed to survive thirty-six-hour shifts at the hospital during her intern days. That wasn't exactly a century ago.

"Okay," she surrendered, "if you promise to have a sandwich ready for me, I'll be by your apartment in a half hour. Lucky for you I've got a little black dress stashed in my supply closet for just these kinds of emergencies."

Natalya waited for the inevitable onslaught of backhanded gratitude that Clancy had turned into an art form. When it failed to materialize, she had no idea what to make of it. Was he pouting? Was something wrong?

"Clancy, say something," she ordered.

"Come. Please."

Each word sounded more like steam escaping from a faulty radiator in the dead of winter than something that had actually been spoken.

An uneasiness undulated through her, but she banked it down. "Clancy, if this is your idea of a joke, it's not funny."

Clancy was not beyond playing practical jokes. She had always thought that it was his way of dealing with the fact that he earned a living by working in a mortuary. She knew it couldn't exactly be pleasant, having to deal with grieving people and dead bodies every day.

That and—in contrast to her own home life, which was the last word in warmth—Clancy's childhood had been one with which Dickens could have sympathized.

He looked like a walking victim, something that he was with a fair amount of regularity. Until Natalya had come into his life.

When Clancy made no response to her words, she suddenly asked, "Are you sick?"

Instead of saying yes or no, she heard him repeat the word "Come," weakly.

In the background, she heard a noise, like a loud bang. And then there was nothing. The connection disappeared.

Had she lost the signal, or had something happened to Clancy? She didn't want her mind going there, but he wasn't the type to carry a joke too far.

"Hello? Hello? Clancy, if this is your stupid idea of a joke…" she said, clinging to the hope that it was. She'd rush off to his apartment, thinking the worst, and Clancy would be there in that almost threadbare tuxedo he insisted on wearing to gallery openings, waiting for her. And grinning that lopsided grin of his.

At which point she wouldn't know whether

to hug him with relief or beat on him with both fists for scaring her.

She stood and debated her next move. Hot tub, or Clancy's apartment.

With a silent promise to herself to read him the riot act once she found him alive and well, she chose Clancy's apartment. Natalya quickly changed into the dress she kept on hand for last-minute invitations to hospital fund-raisers and the occasional unexpected date that came upon her like a diamond in the rough.

She was dressed, out of the office and heading toward the elevator in less than five minutes. Adrenaline was pumping through her veins even though she told herself that there was nothing to worry about and that Clancy was fine.

She was still telling herself that when she was standing outside of Clancy's small apartment some twenty-five minutes later. She knocked on his door, but he didn't answer. Not then, nor the second time that her knuckles rapped against the door.

She could feel her palms growing slightly damp.

"Clancy," Natalya said under her breath, "I swear I'm going to wring your skinny neck if you're doing this to get even with me for trying to beg off," she promised more to hearten herself than to threaten him.

Beneath it all was an uneasy feeling that something was very wrong.

"Enough with being polite," she announced, digging into her purse. She took out her key to Clancy's apartment, which he had given her in case of emergencies.

"I think this qualifies as an emergency," she said out loud, as if Clancy was standing at her elbow. "And when I find you standing there, smirking, you're going to see just how much of an emergency you have on your hands. Please be there, smirking," she added, turning the key.

When she opened the door, there was no one there. Her heart sank down into the pit of her stomach.

It took less than thirty seconds to scan the living room. The same amount for the bedroom, and the bathroom door was standing open, allowing her to see in. Clancy wasn't anywhere. This wasn't like him. He never forgot an appointment. Not even once.

The uneasiness that had been moving through her was now racing in her veins.

Something was very wrong.

Now that she thought about it, he'd told her how much he wanted to see this particular artist, saying that he could relate to the man's angst. He wouldn't be wasting time like this, he'd want to get to the art gallery.

Taking out her cell phone, Natalya quickly pressed the number to Clancy's phone. The second she finished, she heard a busy signal pulsating against her ear. It had that peculiar rhythm that phones had when they weren't properly disconnected.

Had he left his phone on?

Or had it been taken away from him before he could properly end his call? It was no secret that Clancy could annoy people. Had someone decided to take out their annoyance on Clancy?

"Take it easy, Nat," she told herself. "He's probably still at work." She knew that his boss, Walter Tolliver, didn't allow his employees to have cell phones on while on the premises.

That made more sense, she thought. She'd just been overreacting. It had been years since someone had decided to attempt to rearrange Clancy's face because of something he'd said.

Pausing a second to remember the number of the mortuary's landline, she pressed the corresponding buttons on her keypad.

He was probably still there, she reassured herself again. More than likely, Tolliver was having him work overtime. The newly appointed funeral parlor director clearly didn't like Clancy. He made things as difficult as possible for her friend, undoubtedly hoping that if things were uncomfortable enough, he'd quit. What the man hadn't reckoned on was Clancy's stubbornness.

"Ellis Brothers Mortuary," a deep, resonant and cultured voice announced. She wasn't expecting to hear Tolliver's voice. "How may I assist you in your time of grief?"

Natalya'd met the man once and had taken an instant dislike to him. But then, her viewpoint might have been slightly tainted, she mused with a half smile. She'd always felt like Clancy's big sister instead of just his friend.

"Mr. Tolliver, this is Dr. Natalya Pulaski. May I speak to Clancy?"

"I'm sorry, he's not here." She could almost visualize the man stiffening as he frowned. "He left for the evening."

Ordinarily, that would be what she'd thought. But since she was standing in the middle of Clancy's apartment and he wasn't there, she had no choice but to assume he was still being kept at work. There weren't that many places that Clancy frequented. Outside of her apartment and her parents' house, there was a restaurant he liked to go to with her. "Are you sure?"

"Very." Tolliver's tone told her that the man was offended at having his answer questioned.

Right now, she didn't care about Tolliver's feelings. She wanted to find Clancy. "Would you happen to know what time he left?"

"He clocked out at five," Tolliver informed her crisply. "Why?" he wanted to know, though his manner was impersonal. "Is there a problem?"

Yes, there's a problem, Natalya thought. *Clancy's disappeared.*

She frowned, going over the little pieces of information that she knew. If Clancy left the mortuary at five, there was no reason why he wouldn't be home right now. And yet, he wasn't.

So where was he? she wondered. And why had he sounded so odd when he'd called? Why hadn't he said anything more?

Because she knew that Tolliver was waiting for a response she said, "Clancy was supposed to meet me for a gallery opening tonight."

"I'm afraid your friend feels that mundane things such as time do not apply to him," Tolliver told her. She heard him give a dismissive snort. "He'll turn up. If he doesn't," he added with an air of superiority that she found extremely offensive, "I'd consider myself lucky."

Hot words hovered on the tip of her tongue, but she bit them back. "Well, you're not me, Mr. Tolliver. And I'd say that was fortunate for both of us." Natalya didn't bother saying goodbye when she broke the connection.

If she'd been moderately worried before, she was really worried now.

Chapter 2

"Hot date tonight?"

Detective Michael DiPalma closed his locker door only to find his partner, Louis Rawlings, filling the space where, minutes ago, no one had stood. Considering the man's portly build, he moved with the speed and quiet of a stealth bomber.

At the moment, Louis was grinning wistfully, waiting for an answer to his question.

"No," Mike finally answered.

Mike gave his locker a quick tug to make sure that the lock had taken. The PDA where he kept all his important phone numbers had gone missing for several days before it had been mysteriously returned. He was taking no chances this time.

Like a puppy denied a favorite toy, Louis's jovial expression sagged around the edges until it was almost hangdog in appearance. "But, Mike, it's Friday."

Mike placed his motorcycle helmet beside him on the bench to fix the cuff of his jeans. "I'm aware of what day of the week it is, Louis."

"You always have a hot date on Fridays."

Mike straightened and got up. "Now you're exaggerating."

Louis shook his head. Fringes of carefully preserved hair moved from side to side. "No, that's for you to do. But you do it so well that it seems real." Brown eyes looked at him eagerly. "C'mon, Mike, you're the only fantasy life I have."

Lips that were just as quick to frown as they were to smile curved tolerantly as he looked at the shorter man. "You're married, Lou."

"My point exactly." The sentence was accompanied by a large, pronounced sigh.

With a laugh, Mike zipped up his leather jacket. His motorcycle was waiting for him and all he wanted to do tonight was get on it and head for his one-bedroom apartment. "Jackie is supposed to fulfill all your fantasies."

Louis stared at him in wonder as they began to walk out of the locker room together. "Have you *seen* Jackie lately?" He stopped a moment, holding his hand up approximately five feet from the floor. "Small woman, surrounded by yelling kids?" He dropped his hand and sighed again. "I can't even get near her."

"What you need is a night out with your wife, Rawlings," Mike advised. He firmly believed that every woman needed a little romance in her life. Especially a wife. To allay the skeptical expression on Louis's face, Mike offered his partner the services of his youngest sister. "Claudia would be happy to babysit for you some time."

Though he'd never been married, he knew what it was like to be in the center of a large family. His own had six, not counting his mother and father, or his grandmother when she'd lived with them. There were four boys in his family and two girls. And throughout all the ups and downs, good times and bad, his parents had managed to maintain a loving relationship.

Which was why they had so many kids, he mused.

His family was the reason behind his easy-going manner, as they had shown him by example that there was nothing that couldn't be handled given time and the right approach. They were also responsible for his wanting to enjoy himself as much as possible before he finally settled down and committed to one woman.

If he ever settled down and committed to one woman, he qualified silently. So far, none of the women he'd gone out with remotely filled the requirements he had for a life partner.

Josephine and Salvatore DiPalma had married straight out of high school and become parents nine months to the day of their anniversary. Though both said they wouldn't change a thing and regretted nothing, Mike doubted if that was a hundred percent true. They'd gone from being children to having children, never taking time to be carefree, to be young.

That wasn't going to be the way he intended to play it. There were a whole lot of things in life he wanted to do and see before settling down and facing things like mortgages and pediatrician bills.

Holding open the door that led to the stairwell, Mike glanced at his partner. Louis was obviously chewing on what he'd just said.

"A night out, huh?" Louis echoed.

Mike shrugged carelessly. "Night out, night in. You could check into a hotel with Jackie and pretend you're not married."

"That would take a lot of pretending." But it was obvious by the look in his eyes that Louis was warming to the idea.

Mike laughed and clapped him on the back. "My money's on you."

But Louis clearly didn't want to dwell on his own humdrum life, even if a date with his wife was in the not-too-distant future.

"So, what's with you?" he wanted to know. "No Shelley tonight? Wait, it's not Shelley anymore, is it? It's Judith." He shook his head again. "Or was that Lisa?"

It was Elaine, but he wasn't about to add another name to the mix. Despite all of Louis's urgings, he was not the type who believed in disclosing intimate details of an evening. A lady deserved her privacy and he treated all the women he went out with like ladies. His up-bringing demanded nothing less.

"All history," Mike told him.

By design, after Brenda, his relationships were all pleasant and light. "Like a diet cookie with all the good things taken out," his mother had once assessed in her concern that her secondborn would not follow in his older brother's footsteps and find a woman to start a family with. "No substance, no flavor."

After nearly making a fatal mistake and reaching the altar with a woman who was all wrong for him, light and pleasant was just the way he wanted it. As far as he was concerned, his relationships had just enough substance. He and the women he dated never got too serious and enjoyed each other's company until it was time to move on.

And he moved on a lot. With no regrets. He enjoyed women's company, and in turn, he made sure that they enjoyed his.

Mike had a sneaking suspicion that they also enjoyed the danger he represented. The gun and his line of work generated that kind of aura. And women were drawn to it like the proverbial flies to honey. It was a double whammy, his other sister, Theresa, had once told him. If his tall, dark, handsome looks hadn't been enough to draw women to him, the nature of his work sealed the bargain.

He tended to make women feel safe at the same time that he took their breath away. And every woman in his life knew that her position was temporary. No lies were told, no promises given. And a good time was had by all.

A good time that sent his partner's imagination into overtime.

But tonight he was tired. Tomorrow was his nephew Alan's first birthday and Mike's parents were going all out to celebrate it. They lived in Brooklyn, in the same house they'd moved into thirty-six years ago. It was located in the center of an Italian community where everyone believed in celebrating in a big way. He'd already given his promise to be there. Nursing a hangover was not the way he wanted to greet his mother for the first time in almost three weeks. The lectures about how he was wasting the best years of his life would be endless and unendurable.

"So there's someone new?" Louis asked hopefully. Like a junkyard dog, when Louis clamped down on something, it was hard to make him let go.

"Not at the moment." Reaching the first floor, Mike walked ahead of Louis to the door and exited the stairwell. He looked over his shoulder at his partner and flashed a grin. "But you'll be the first to know when there is, Lou. Until then, I'm—"

And then he saw her.

A vivacious-looking, petite woman with

dark red hair that swirled about her like a cloud absorbing rays from a setting sun. At the moment, she looked frustrated and distraught.

Not that he could blame her. She was talking to Mulroney, the desk sergeant, a man who was not known for his patient, under-standing manner. Mulroney's forte was paper, not people.

Louis looked from his partner to the woman Mike was staring at. The woman who had stolen the second half of Mike's sentence before it had a chance to come out.

A knowing smile slipped over Louis's small lips. "My guess is that I'm already looking at her," he murmured under his breath.

Mike heard only a buzz of words. His atten-tion was suddenly riveted to the woman before Mulroney's tall, scarred desk.

"Lady, I already told you—come back in

forty-eight hours." Dismissing her, the hulking sergeant looked down at the stack of papers before him.

If he meant to get rid of her that easily, he was in for a surprise, Natalya thought. Not her mother's daughter for nothing, she dug in. "It's 'doctor,' not 'lady,'" she corrected him tersely. "And I'm telling you that I know Clancy. Something's wrong. He wouldn't just disappear this way."

Mike drew closer. Ordinarily, he tried not to get into Mulroney's face. He had enough cases to work, enough on his plate not to look for one more serving. Mike knew he should just keep moving until he reached his motorcycle and the beginning of his weekend.

But he liked the way the woman wasn't letting Mulroney intimidate her. And she did sound genuinely concerned. He was good about first impressions and his first impression of her was that she wasn't rattled easily.

"Something I can help with?" he offered mildly, looking from the desk sergeant to the woman standing before him.

The woman was dressed with neither precision nor carelessness. It struck him that her clothing adhered lovingly to her form, as if trying to please herself and not with the intent to catch attention. But she did anyway. He saw the way Louis was eyeing her. As if she were a fantasy being served up hot on a plate.

Mike moved his six-foot-one frame between the woman and his shorter partner, blocking Louis's view. And his unabashed stare.

"She's trying to file a missing person's report, but the guy's only been missing a few hours, if that," Mulroney complained, irritated. "I told her that she had to come back when it was official. He could have just stepped out for a beer," Mulroney added, looking at Louis since it was obvious that Mike wasn't paying attention to what he was saying.

Mike's attention was fully focused on the woman. She had green eyes he noticed. He'd always liked green eyes.

"Husband?" he guessed respectfully. But even as the word was out of his mouth, he glanced down at her left hand and saw that there was no band there. No engagement ring, either. He felt his interest sharpening. What was her connection to the missing man?

Natalya shook her head. "Friend."

She'd come down to the precinct because she knew that calling the police would have been futile. They would have just told her to call back. Apparently coming in person was yielding the same results. When she'd become concerned about Clancy, her initial thought had been to call Sash's fiancé, Tony. He was a detective with NYPD and she knew he would help.

But Sasha had taken a rare day off and gone with Tony to Atlantic City for a short three-day holiday, something she'd never remembered her sister doing. Of all of them, Sasha was the most intense one. The one who had been most driven. And now she was making a conscious effort to enjoy the good moments that life sent. Her first fiancé had been killed right in front of her, and since luck and love had smiled on her a second time, her older sister was putting nothing off until tomorrow.

Which was wonderful for Sasha, but didn't help her any.

In her gut, Natalya knew, just knew, that something was wrong. That Clancy was in trouble and needed rescuing. But explaining something like that to the burly sergeant behind the desk was something she knew would fall on deaf ears. Maybe she'd have more luck with this good-looking knight in shining armor. She'd always had luck with good-looking men, she thought, hoping that it would hold.

The surly desk sergeant was making his case to the man who had asked if he could help. "She said the guy had called her just a little while ago, croaking out some message."

Incensed at the dismissive manner in which the sergeant repeated her words, Natalya turned toward the tall newcomer.

"He didn't croak, he sounded as if he couldn't talk. Like he was hurt and forcing the words out," she emphasized. "I know something's happened to him. We were supposed to go to this art gallery opening tonight. He was very excited about it. Clancy wouldn't just miss that."

The dark-haired man nodded, his expression thoughtful. As if he were listening to every nuance. "Have you tried him at home?"

"Yes, I'm not an idiot—" Natalya stopped herself abruptly as her words replayed themselves in her ears. She sounded like a shrew. But then, that was because she was so worried. "Sorry, that came out too short. I went over to Clancy's apartment," she continued in a voice she struggled to keep calm. "I have a key. He wasn't there."

"Were any of his clothes gone?" the man she assumed was a detective asked.

Chagrined, Natalya mentally cursed herself for the oversight.

"I didn't think to look." She looked up at this new person on the scene, waiting for some criticism. When it didn't come, she glanced at the shorter man beside him. His partner? She had no idea, but the more people she got on her side, the faster Clancy could be found. "He wouldn't just run out on me," she protested, wanting the taller man to know the reason for her concern, "especially without an explanation—"

"Did you have an argument?" Mike pressed. A lot of people just overlooked the obvious, allowing their emotions to carry them away and create mountains when there weren't even any anthills in sight. "Sometimes a lovers' quarrel can—"

"We're not lovers," Natalya interrupted. "I already told you that Clancy's my friend." Natalya took a breath. "We've been friends since elementary school. I'm probably the only friend he has," she added.

It wasn't something she would have readily

admitted. Saying as much was being unfair to Clancy. It allowed others to know how difficult it was for Clancy to make any friends. For the most part, he turned people off. She was very protective of him, but the uneasiness she felt about Clancy's state overruled things like secrets and maintaining his right to privacy.

"He called me on my cell phone and when I answered, his exact words were 'Come. Please.' That's all." She looked from one detective to the other. "It sounded as if he was pushing the words out, as if he was having trouble talking. Trouble breathing," she added for emphasis.

Her eyes never left the taller of the two men. He looked neither amused nor annoyed. She took heart that maybe she'd found the right man to help her.

"Is he prone to playing tricks on you?" the man asked.

"No." It was a lie, a small white lie. Clancy had played a few tricks on her over the years, but for the most part, they'd been inconsequential. This was no time to drag up feebly executed practical jokes from the past. She knew that all her concerns would be summarily dismissed if she did. "I just know something's happened to him."

Although she wasn't looking at Mulroney, she heard the desk sergeant utter a dismissive huff. She began to get desperate. Just the way Clancy had to feel when he made that call to her, she thought. "Look, don't you people have ways of tracking a cell phone if it's on?"

"Yeah."

It was the first time she heard the man beside the tall detective say anything and she looked to this new avenue of hope.

"Who do I have to talk to in order for that to

happen?" she wanted to know, addressing him. An urgency had slipped into her voice. She just couldn't get herself to shake the feeling that, for Clancy, time was running out.

"You don't," Mike told her. She looked at him sharply. He could see that she was about to protest. He'd bet she could hold her own in an argument. "I do."

Mulroney leaned over the desk, "I thought you were off the clock," the desk sergeant reminded him. Raising one stubby forefinger, he deliberately pointed to the clock on the far wall.

"You know better than that, Sergeant," Mike told him pleasantly. "A New York City policeman is never off the clock." Before Mulroney could say anything further, Mike turned toward the woman who had initiated all this. His helmet in the crook of his left arm, he put out his hand to her. "I'm Detective Michael

DiPalma." Because he heard Louis shift beside him, he added, "And this is my partner, Detective Louis Rawlings." He spared a glance toward the shorter man. "It's okay, Louis. I can take it from here. Go home to Jackie and the kids. Tell them I said hello."

Louis's face fell. But it was late and he'd already confided to Mike that he'd promised Jackie not to stop off for a beer before going home. Since he lived in Queens, under perfect conditions, his journey home would take him approximately a half hour. Jackie tended to be aware of the clock.

He leaned in to his partner before leaving. "Call me," he instructed Mike. And then he nodded at the woman he would have bet a month's pay was destined to be his partner's newest love interest. She was far too well put together, with long, shapely legs, for Mike to simply ignore once he did what he could to help her.

Louis inclined his head in her direction. "I hope you find your friend."

Natalya smiled. The man sounded genuine, not like the desk sergeant. Mentally, she crossed her fingers. Maybe she was overreacting. Maybe this was all a tempest in a teapot and Clancy would turn up. But somehow, she doubted it.

"I certainly hope so," she replied. "I certainly hope so."

With one last lingering look over his shoulder, Louis mumbled his goodbye to Mike and went on his way. The desk sergeant awarded them one last, exasperated glance and then returned to the report that had been the focus of his attention when Natalya had walked in.

She felt the uneasiness in the pit of her stomach settle slightly. The detective took her elbow and guided her toward one of the benches that ran along the side of the wall facing the desk sergeant.

"First order of business," he began once they were seated, "is for you to tell me your name."

There was something about the way he said it that had Natalya temporarily wondering if she'd made a mistake coming here and not trying to track Tony down to ask for help. The next moment, she told herself she was being paranoid and banked down the feeling.

She put out her hand to him. "I'm Dr. Natalya Pulaski."

"Pulaski," he repeated as if he was already familiar with the name. "You're kidding, right?"

Chapter 3

Natalya looked at him for a second. What an odd thing to say. "Why would I kid about something like that?"

Now that he thought of it, Vinnie had said something about Carol's doctor being a knockout, but he hadn't paid much attention. Vinnie was definitely guilty of understatement.

"You are Dr. Pulaski?" He realized how dumb that probably sounded to her, but for the most part, he was a man who didn't believe in coincidences. Yet what else could this be?

Natalya looked at him a little uncertainly. She'd just said as much. Maybe she should have tried harder to find Sasha's fiancé. Good-looking or not, Detective Mike DiPalma might not exactly be the sharpest scalpel on the surgical tray.

"Yes. Why?"

He grinned and a ripple went through her that, had this been any other time or occasion, she would have recognized for what it was—pure, unadulterated chemistry. "You delivered my brother Vinnie's baby last year."

For a second, despite the anxiety that was steadily mounting within her stomach, Natalya allowed herself a slight smile. This happened every so often. People not only confused her with Sasha, but with Kady, as well. Once her last two sisters were ready to hang out their shingles, there'd be no end to the confusion. It wasn't exactly the most common name in the book.

Natalya shook her head. "No, I didn't."

Mike didn't follow. She'd just said she was a doctor. "But—"

"That was my sister. Sasha," Natalya clarified before he could ask any more questions. "She's the ob-gyn in the family."

In his family, everyone had different occupations. He couldn't imagine any of his brothers being on the force. "There are two of you?"

"Actually—" Natalya's smile widened "—there're five of us."

He stared at her, a little stunned. Two doctors in the family was somewhat unusual. Five was close to unbelievable. "Five doctors?"

Natalya inclined her head. "Doctors or almost-doctors."

At any other time, she might have enjoyed this. Enjoyed talking to a man who was good-looking enough to knock the socks off a barefoot woman. Enjoyed exchanging personal data, piece by piece, like some sort of trade of vital information.

But right now, she couldn't seem to still the uneasy feeling inside her that Clancy was in trouble. And that he needed her. She was the only one who could help him. Or cared enough to help him. She was fairly confident that his mother wouldn't even notice he was missing until it was too late.

So it was up to her to make sure that it didn't get to that point.

"I'll introduce you to the whole lot of them," she suddenly promised. "*After* we find Clancy."

The use of the pronoun stood out in ten-foot letters. He had to set her straight before this got out of hand. As a rule, civilians were not included in police business. The rule was rarely broken.

"There is no 'we,' Doc," he informed her quickly. He saw her look at him in surprise. "You give me as much information as you think will help, including his cell phone number, and I'll see what I can do." There was a favor he could call in that might solve everything, he thought.

The look on the doctor's face told him that Natalya had other ideas on the matter. "This isn't official, is it?" she asked.

Mulroney had it right. Her friend wasn't considered a missing person until more time had gone by. There was only one exception to that rule. "Not unless your friend is under twelve."

"Then if it's not official police business yet, I can come with you. Clancy might be hurt." God knew he sounded as if he was when he'd called. "And I'm a doctor," she reminded Mike.

It occurred to him that he didn't know what discipline she practiced. For all he knew, she could be a psychiatrist, which wouldn't be very helpful unless her friend was suffering from hysterical amnesia. "What kind of a doctor?"

"A good one." The answer evoked a tolerant smile. She knew he was still waiting for an answer he could work with. "A pediatrician."

"Little people." His tone told her that he didn't see that as exactly being very useful in the present situation.

"Who are often treated for the same things as big people—and more." Natalya straightened her shoulders. "I can be helpful," she insisted.

Mike looked at her, debating whether or not to relent. He was not unaware that the desk sergeant was periodically eyeing them both. He hated having anyone looking over his shoulder. It had led to more than one fight when he was a kid. Before he found other ways to handle things than with his fists.

Mike rose to his feet. The doctor followed suit. "All right, come upstairs with me. You can give me some information about this Clancy and I can see if I can get a location on him for you."

The suggestion got him a smile that was the closest thing to lethal he'd seen in a very long time.

"Thank you."

He began to lead the way to the rear of the building. "Don't thank me yet. We haven't found him."

They would, she thought. *They had to.* "But you're looking."

Her gratitude embarrassed him, which was a first.

Instead of taking the stairwell, the way he always did, Mike opted for the elevator. When

he pressed for the car, the doors opened immediately. The ride up gave him a sufficient
amount of time to get the information he
needed about her missing friend. As they
stepped out of the elevator, Natalya took a photograph out of her wallet and passed it to him.

"Clancy?" It was a rhetorical question. The
man looked rather unremarkable. His expression was almost self-conscious, Mike thought.
He held on to the photograph as he led the way
down the corridor to the squad room he'd
vacated less than a half hour ago.

"It's the most recent photograph I have of
him," she said.

He nodded. "That'll help. If it gets to that."

She wanted to ask him what he meant by that,
but held her tongue. She didn't want him to
think she was being antagonistic in any way.
After all, he was going out of his way to help her.

Natalya made herself as comfortable as possible in the small glass-walled cubicle within the squad room that smelled of musty papers, mustier sweat and Pine-Sol. The weekly cleaning crew had apparently just been through here. Not a shred of paper resided in any of the wastebaskets.

She watched as the detective made a phone call. She saw him smile as he managed to catch whoever it was he was calling. The broad-shouldered man created a hell of an imposing impression, she thought.

Mike could picture the annoyed look on Caleb Brown's face once hellos were exchanged and he'd identified himself. It wasn't that they didn't get along. Caleb's mind clocked out the moment his day ended. He didn't like putting in a minute of extra time.

"Need a favor, Caleb."

"I'm meeting friends at the Watering Hole," the deep voice over the phone protested, referring to the bar and grill where tired, overworked police personnel let off a little steam before going home and trying to fit back into their private lives.

"The friends and the Watering Hole will keep," Mike assured him. He could hear another protest in the making as Caleb drew in his breath. "Unless you want a certain story about you and what happened in the evidence room to make the rounds...." He let his voice trail off. It'd been his good fortune to walk in on Caleb and the officer in charge of the evidence room. Officer Serena Daly filled out her uniform more pleasingly than most.

Mike heard the creak of a chair. Caleb had sat back down again. "Okay, okay, what d'you need?"

"I need a trace done on a cell phone."

"Only works if the phone is on," Caleb told him tersely.

Mike glanced at Natalya. Caleb's voice was loud enough to carry, even though the receiver was against his ear. She nodded. "We're thinking it is."

"Okay," Caleb reluctantly surrendered, "what's the number?"

Mike read off what the woman with the killer legs had given him, starting with the 718 area code.

"Got it." There was no mistaking impatient urgency in Caleb's voice. Mike wondered if he was meeting Officer Daly at the Watering Hole. "Give me a minute."

"Take as many minutes as you need, Caleb," Mike told him.

"Very generous of you," Caleb retorted

sourly. The sound of typing and then more typing was heard as the man on the other end triangulated the signal associated with the cell phone number he'd been given. "This program is amazing," Mike heard him murmuring under his breath. The last keystroke sounded as if finger met keyboard with a flourish. "Got it!"

The declaration was followed by silence served in a container. "Would you like to share what you just found with the class?" Mike coaxed.

"Does this get me off the hook?" Caleb wanted to know.

Unlike Caleb, he wasn't about to be bartered with. "We'll talk," Mike promised.

The man on the other end sighed loudly. "DiPalma, I can't go through life with you holding that over my head."

He would have thought by now Caleb would

have realized that he really wasn't the type to point fingers—or ruin a man's marriage.

"You won't, I promise." He glanced at the woman sitting by his desk. She was on the edge of her seat and looked ready to spring up to her feet. He caught himself wondering what she'd be like in bed, then pushed the thought to the side. "Now, if you don't mind, what's the address?"

"Looks to me like the guy you're after is in Soho." Caleb recited a more precise address.

Mike wrote it down, then nodded. "Thanks. One more thing, is he moving?"

There was a pause. "Doesn't look like it," Caleb said finally. Mike heard the sound of the computer being closed down for the night before another request could be made. "So when do you finally owe me?"

He could have told him that they were even, but that meant that he'd have to resort to something else whenever he needed a little extra help under the table. The police department was strangling itself with red tape these days and he had neither the patience nor the temperament to play along a hundred percent of the time.

"Next early frost in June—we'll talk about it then." Mike broke the connection before the inevitable barage of words flowed out to bury him. Caleb could be extremely long-winded when he felt the occasion warranted it.

Turning, Mike handed the address he'd just written down to Natalya. "Looks like Clancy went to that opening without you."

"He wouldn't do that," she insisted defensively. And then she looked down at the paper and actually read the address. She shook her head. "This wasn't the place. We weren't going there." But she was going there now, she thought. Folding the paper, she rose to her feet. She held it up for a second before pocketing it. "Thank you for this."

Mike pushed back his chair and rose. He made the natural assumption. "You going down there?"

She saw no reason to deny it. This was why she'd come in the first place. To find out where Clancy was. If Clancy turned out to be all right, she was going to read him the riot act. Just before she pounded on his head. "Yes."

He'd thought as much. "You have a way to get down there?" he asked as he escorted her out of the small cubicle.

Like Sasha, she had a car. Unlike Sasha, she rarely used hers. She tended to be preoccupied, not the best state in which to drive a vehicle. "New York City has a great transit system," she commented.

The doctor didn't look like the type to hang

on a bus strap, or sandwich herself between people on a subway car. "I'm still off duty," he reminded her. "I'll give you a ride."

Natalya hesitated. He'd already done so much, she didn't want to put him out any further. Besides, if Clancy did turn out to be all right, he'd be chagrined by all the fuss. He didn't mind a fuss being made, but for the right reason and privately.

It was on the tip of her tongue to say she could handle it from here. But somehow, she heard herself saying, "That would be very nice of you." Just in case, she added silently, everything *wasn't* all right.

Glancing over his shoulder as he held the elevator door open for her, Mike flashed a grin that accentuated two deep dimples, one in each cheek. "My mother says I'm a nice kind of guy."

She stepped in and the doors closed. "I think mothers are obligated to say things like that. My mother says the same thing about me."

Amusement highlighted his blue eyes. "That you're a nice guy?"

"No." She laughed. "That I'm a nice girl."

In the corridor now, he glanced at her just before he opened the main front door. "I think your mother's probably an excellent judge."

For one of the few times in her life, Natalya was at a loss for a comeback. Fortunately, she didn't have to say anything because they had just stopped by a motorcycle parked right in front of the precinct. The detective took a lock off the rear wheel.

"This is your ride?" She tried not to sound as incredulous as she felt.

Mike nodded. He ran a loving hand over the visor. "Has been ever since college."

"What does your mother have to say about that?"

Josephine DiPalma had been far from thrilled the day he rode the bike home. But he was over eighteen and it had been purchased with his own money. There was little she could do except cross herself and pray.

"That I'm going to wind up breaking every bone in my body. She'd be thrilled if she knew I'd just met a doctor whose mother thinks she's a nice girl." It was a teasing remark, with more than a little truth at the bottom. His mother would have loved nothing more than to have him bring a physician home and announce his engagement right then and there.

And then he became serious. "If you'd rather not—" Mike nodded at the motorcycle, his meaning clear "—I could sign out one of the department's cars and take you in that—"

But she shook her head. The motorcycle had surprised her, but it hadn't displeased her. "I love motorcycles," she told him. Her expression was soft as she added, "I like to feel the wind in my hair."

"No wind in hair," Mike countered. There were times when he took chances, but they didn't include his motorcycle, or people he allowed to accompany him on the bike. Opening the black leather case strapped across the rear of the seat, he took out a spare helmet and handed it to Natalya.

Her eyes smiled as she accepted the helmet. "You're not as daring as you look."

Strapping the helmet on, she got on the motorcycle behind him. She tucked her arms around the detective's waist, lacing her fingers together, leaning in closer to keep from falling off.

Mike revved up his motor. Looking up, he saw Caleb exiting the building. The software tech looked in his direction and their eyes met. The expression on the other man's face was decidedly envious. He pointed toward her and mouthed the words "That one." Mike knew that he was asking to be introduced to Natalya.

Some people, he decided, were just incorrigible. They also never learned.

He figured Caleb wasn't going to readily believe him when he got around to telling the man that the redhead leaning into him with her arms around his waist was not his date.

For a Friday evening, crosstown traffic was not as heavy as it could have been. Weaving his motorcycle in and out between lanes of cars with the ease of a tailor plying his needle, Mike managed to make amazing time. They reached the gallery in less than twenty minutes from the moment they left the curb.

The gallery was hardly more than a storefront. It was wedged in between a trendy restaurant and a store that sold overpriced shoes. There was a sign that proclaimed that there was more parking in the rear. Since both sides of the one-way street were filled to capacity, not even leaving space for a prayer, Mike had no choice. He followed the once white, now weather-beaten arrow halfway down the block, turned right and then snaked his way down a narrow passage that had been built before things such as SUVs had captured the country's fancy.

When he pulled his motorbike into the lot, Mike looked around. The lot attendant was nowhere to be found. Never hesitating, Mike made his way into the heart of the semiempty lot, choosing a place that was close to the gallery's rear door. As he waited for the woman behind him to release her hold and get off, Mike felt her body stiffen against his back. He heard a sharp, pained intake of breath behind him.

"What's the matter?" Squinting, he looked around to see what had upset her.

Natalya didn't answer. Instead, she jumped off the bike. Turning around, Mike saw her running to the other end of the lot.

A streetlamp in the middle of the block was casting an irregular pool of light just within the confines of the small lot.

"Doc?" he called after her.

Natalya heard a faint noise behind her, but she didn't turn around to acknowledge it. She was completely focused on what she'd thought she saw several yards away.

Boots.

Boots sticking up from under the nose of a parked vehicle. She wouldn't have noticed, except that the light from the streetlamp had caught just the tips and illuminated them.

White boots.

Like the kind Clancy liked to wear. It was a pair she'd given him for Christmas one year. White boots in lieu of a white hat. It was a reference to her calling him a good guy, like the kind who lived in old-fashioned Westerns and dressed all in white.

As she hurried to the site, Natalya prayed it was just her overwrought imagination, playing tricks on her eyes.

But even as she quickened her pace, she knew she wasn't wrong.

And then she saw him. Wearing that silly tuxedo he liked to put on for openings. A tuxedo with white boots. An outfit guaranteed to get him noticed. He was lying on the ground beside a car, a strange, strangled expression on his face.

"Clancy?" she cried out loud, then raised her voice, calling his name again, trying to rouse him. To get him to sit up and tell her everything was all right. That he'd just fainted, or gotten dizzy or even passed out, drunk. Except that Clancy didn't drink.

But Clancy didn't sit up, didn't stir. He continued to lie motionless on the ground.

Sick to her stomach, Natalya dropped to her knees beside him just as Mike caught up to her. Frantically, she felt for Clancy's pulse. First at his wrist, then at his throat.

There was none.

Horrified, she placed her hand less than half an inch from his nose. There wasn't even the faintest indication of breath.

She felt a tightness in her chest, constricting it. With effort, she banked it down and immediately began to administer CPR. Tears began to sting her eyes but she didn't stop to wipe them away. She couldn't afford to. Every second counted.

"Dammit, Clancy," Natalya cried angrily at the immobile figure on the ground before her. "What have you gotten yourself into this time?"

Standing over her, Mike had a better view of the situation. A better view of the ashen pallor of the man's face. He knew that no matter what the extent of her medical training was, it wouldn't allow Natalya to bring her friend around.

The man was dead.

Chapter 4

Natalya remained kneeling by the body, holding Clancy's lifeless hand until the ambulance arrived.

Mike had called for the ambulance rather than the coroner's wagon because he wanted someone other than Natalya to pronounce her friend dead. When the two attendants prepared to place Clancy within the black body bag, he gently took hold of her shoulders and brought her to her feet.

Her face was almost as ashen as the face of the man being zipped into the bag.

"Why don't I have someone take you home?" Mike said quietly.

The suggestion made Natalya come back to life. She looked at him and shook her head. "No, I'm going with Clancy in the ambulance." She looked beyond his head, toward where the attendants were placing the gurney in the van. Natalya moved to follow. "I don't want him to go alone."

Mike placed a hand on her shoulder, not so much to restrain her as to give her human contact. "He's past knowing, Doc," he told her gently.

She looked at him with eyes that held so much emotion, Mike found himself completely captivated by her.

"He'll know," she replied so softly, it would have been easy to miss the conviction had he not been straining to hear her.

After a beat, Mike nodded his approval to the attendant. The latter shrugged and made room for Natalya in the back beside the gurney.

Natalya got in, but before she sat down, she leaned forward and unzipped the bag just a little past Clancy's clavicle.

About to climb into the front passenger seat, the attendant stopped and protested. "Hey."

"Just until we get there," she said.

Neither man could bring himself to argue with her. The attendant shrugged and got into the front of the vehicle.

After several minutes had passed and the silence within the enclosed space grew deafening, Mike finally spoke.

"You're not going to ask to do the autopsy, are you?" Because if she was, that was one debate she wasn't going to be allowed to win.

But if he was waiting for a protest, he didn't receive one. Instead, Natalya looked away from the face of the man she'd befriended since childhood and shook her head.

"No. But I'd like to wait for the results if that's all right."

Mike looked at his watch. On a normal Friday, he would have been home hours ago. His own or whomever he'd gone out with that evening. But here it was, the evening creeping its way to midnight, and he was still technically on the job, debating whether or not he had a homicide on his hands.

Natalya saw him looking at his watch. "You don't have to stay with me. I'll be all right."

He laughed. The woman was something

else. "How long have you had this super-woman complex?"

"Most of my life," she answered without missing a beat. And then her lips moved into a frown. "Some superwoman." She laughed shortly. "I can't even protect a friend."

He wondered what made her feel as if she had to be the dead man's keeper. He saved the question for another time as he pointed out the obvious.

"We don't know yet that this was a homicide. There was no sign of any kind of actual struggle, no bruises or broken neck. Did he have a heart condition?"

She'd made Clancy get a checkup just six months ago, saying that everyone needed one every few years. Clancy had gone reluctantly, only as a favor to her. He'd been in perfect health.

"No."

"Respiratory problems?" When she looked at him, he elaborated. "Like asthma, or allergies. Anaphylactic shock can—"

Natalya cut him short. "Clancy wasn't allergic to anything. Not pollen, peanuts or shellfish. He hardly even ever got a cold."

What he said next caught her off guard. "Then maybe it was a drug overdose."

Pressing her lips together, Natalya shook her head again. "Clancy didn't do drugs."

He'd heard that protest so many times from parents when they were told their child had overdosed. No one ever really knew anyone completely.

"That you know of."

Her eyes narrowed as she looked at him sharply. "Clancy didn't do drugs," she repeated more forcefully. "He didn't even like to take aspirin." Then, in case the detective thought she was trying to deify Clancy, she added, "I've known him most of his life. Clancy was abrasive, he had OCD tendencies and a whole host of other quirks that drove a lot of people up a wall, but he didn't do drugs."

Mike studied her for a long moment. The driver took a turn and he had to quickly brace himself in order not to fall into her.

"And if they find some in his system?"

There was no hesitation on her part. "Then someone must have forced them on him."

What did it take to have someone have that much faith in you, he wondered. "You're sure?"

Again, there was no hesitation. "I'd stake my life on it."

Mike believed her. Believed that *she* believed her friend to be drug free. But whether or not that was the case still remained to be seen.

* * *

"This is going to take time," he warned Natalya once they had reached their destination and Clancy's body had been taken to the autopsy area. "Why don't you go home and I'll have someone call you about the results. *I'll* call you with the results," he amended.

It wasn't that she didn't believe him, but she was far too wound up to get any sleep tonight. At least if she were at the morgue, waiting for the preliminary autopsy results, she'd feel as if she was doing something instead of taking up space.

She took a seat on the bench directly outside the morgue's double doors.

"This is the weekend. I don't have to be anywhere." Which wasn't strictly true. There was Sunday dinner at her parents' house in Queens, but as far as she was concerned that was too far in the future for her to think about right now. "I don't have anything else to do."

A woman as beautiful as you? he thought. He found that hard to believe. With a shrug he sat down beside her in the corridor.

"Don't you have somewhere to be?" she asked him. "You were looking at your watch."

"Habit," he lied. "And if this is a homicide, it'll be mine, so I might as well stick around to find out if it is or not."

She nodded, accepting the explanation. Holding her hands in her lap, she looked straight ahead. "Thank you," she said softly.

Getting to his feet, Mike mumbled something about coffee and went in search of a vending machine.

Back within ten minutes, he had a cup in each hand. She accepted the one he offered her with an absent, grateful smile.

Mike sat down beside her again. He took a long sip of the semicool liquid, then held the paper cup in both hands.

"Is there someone we should be notifying?" he wanted to know. "Next of kin?"

Clancy had been an only child. If there were aunts or uncles, she was certain she would have heard about them. After a moment, she replied, "There's just his mother."

Her jaw had gone rigid, Mike noted. "I'm guessing you don't want to be the one to tell her."

More than once, during her intern days, she'd had to tell family members that their loved one had died. She'd held strangers in her arms and cried with them. But this wasn't that kind of pain.

She raised her chin. "Only because I know it won't matter to her. It might even come as a relief." Without meaning to, she allowed a small, cynical smile to curve her lips. "Until she finds out that he didn't leave her anything."

Fascinated, for more than one reason, Mike never took his eyes from her face. "How would you know that?"

"I'm the executor of his 'estate,' such as it is." Clancy had kidded her about it more than once, but no one was more surprised than she when he'd actually produced a slip of paper he called his will.

Glancing at the detective, she saw an interested look come into his eyes. "It's a joke. Clancy didn't have an 'estate,' he had baseball cards."

"Baseball cards?" Mike echoed. Was she putting him on?

"He collected baseball cards," she explained. Pausing, she took a sip of the coffee he'd brought her, grateful for the gesture. "Had them in mint condition. Never even took them out of the wrapper." She looked at Mike. "I just can't see owning something you love and not handling it."

Why that simple statement made him feel so much warmer than he had a moment ago, Mike didn't know. He attributed the shift to a faulty thermostat in the building's basement, where the morgue was located.

"And he left them to you?"

She took another sip before answering. For a moment, her energy deserted her and she found herself wishing that the coffee was stronger. "His mother would have only thrown them out."

Finishing the unsatisfying coffee, he crushed the cup in his hand and tossed it into the waste-basket some ten feet away. "Tell me more about this mother."

Lucille Donovan was one of the few people

on this earth she intensely disliked. "She's one in name only. Her husband left her years ago. She took it out on Clancy every chance she could, always belittling him, saying that if he were more of a 'regular boy,' his father would have never walked out on them."

"Regular boy?" Mike echoed. He thought he knew what she meant, but he wasn't sure.

Natalya hated the term, but that was what Clancy had told her his mother had said. He'd tried not to look upset, but she knew it was eating him up inside. He blamed himself for his parents' split for years, even though he'd just been seven at the time.

She tried to give the detective as clear a picture as she could. "Clancy didn't play sports, wasn't suave like his father supposedly was. Basically had the word *victim* tattooed on his forehead. Mostly the latter was all Lucille's fault."

Although he had a hunch he knew where this was going, he asked, "Lucille?"

"His mother," Natalya clarified. "They hadn't spoken in five years."

Didn't sound like much of a family unit, Mike thought. But he'd make up his own mind when he got a chance to speak to her. In the meantime, there was something else he wanted to know.

His eyes held hers. "What was your relationship like?"

She knew what he was doing. If one path didn't succeed, he was taking another. But it wouldn't get him to where he thought he was going.

"I was his 'big sister,' although technically, I'm only a month older." She heard what sounded like a workshop saw being turned on and she tried not to imagine what was going on behind the closed doors.

"Anything else?" Mike pressed.

He interrupted her thoughts, bringing her back to their conversation. "Such as?"

"Something more intimate?"

The one note he was strumming was getting tiresome. "I already told you no."

"Fair enough," he acknowledged. "How about him?" The question, he saw, surprised her. "Was he in love with you?"

"He loved me," she qualified slowly, as if measuring her words. "But he wasn't 'in love' with me."

She was making a fine distinction. "And you know this because you're a mind reader?" The question sounded cynical, but he didn't mean it that way.

Her mouth curved again in a semismile, as if she were sharing a joke with herself. "No, I know this because I was the wrong gender. Clancy was

gay. Something else his mother berated him for."
She straightened just a little, turning to face him.
"Look, if you're trying to find out if I had
anything to do with his death—"

"No." He meant that. The stricken look on
her face when they'd found the body had been
spontaneous. The emotion behind it wasn't
something that could have been faked. He'd
had dealings with actresses, both the professional variety and the home-grown drama
queens, and he liked to think that he could tell
a performance from the real thing. There was
always some small, telltale sign that set truth
apart from fiction. "But I'm supposed to ask,"
he leveled with her. "To rule you out."

Natalya got her temper under control, realizing it was just the situation and not the man
that had made her come close to losing it. Detective DiPalma was being as nice as he could,

she thought, especially under the circumstances. She owed him some cooperation.

"Fine, I can appreciate that. I was at my office the entire day. I worked through lunch. Lots of mothers can testify to that. And if that's not enough for you, I've got a priest who can vouch for me."

Was she going to tell him that she ran to confession in between patients? "A priest?"

She nodded. "Father Gannon. He brought in his niece. Her mother—his sister—was sick." She smiled. "We go way back. I knew him when he was Alex Gannon. He's from my old neighborhood," she explained.

The woman was getting more and more intriguing. "You have an interesting circle of friends, Doc. No cops in it?"

She almost laughed, knowing her answer would throw him. "My sister is marrying one.

Sasha. The one who delivered your nephew," she tacked on in case he'd forgotten who Sasha was.

It would have only been natural to have gone to someone she knew first instead of turning up at the station. "Why didn't you ask him to look for your friend?"

"I would have," she said honestly, "but he's out of town." Somewhere in the distance, a door opened and then closed. The sound vibrated down the hall. The morgue was an eerie place at night. "He and Sasha went to Atlantic City." And then she laughed softly to herself. "Figures."

He didn't follow. "Figures?"

It was funny how things turned out, Natalya thought. "Her first vacation since she was two and I wind up needing her fiancé—who's not there."

Well, that answered that question. "So you got me instead."

In response she smiled at him. It wasn't a seductive smile or even a sexy one, but if he'd ever seen a more sensual one he couldn't remember it.

"I got you," she echoed.

His gut tightened. The morgue's thermostat must have went on the fritz again as he was enveloped in warmth.

"I don't believe it," Natalya insisted.

On her feet, she was looking up at the tall, thin man in a smudged lab coat. There was blood on it and she tried not to dwell on where that had come from.

She'd dozed off and had abruptly woken up to the sound of lowered voices. The M.E. had come out and was talking to Mike.

Jumping to her feet, she joined the twosome immediately, only to hear the M.E. tell Mike that a large amount of the latest designer drug that had hit the market had shown up in the tox screen that had been performed on Clancy.

Cause of death was being ascribed to a lethal overdose of the drug.

She caught Mike's arm, making him look at her. "Clancy wouldn't have taken them on his own, Detective. I *know* he wouldn't. Someone had to have made him take it." A thought suddenly hit her. She looked at the M.E. "Was the drug ingested or injected?"

The M.E. glanced at Mike before answering. Mike nodded.

"Injected. There was a small puncture wound in his forearm."

She threw up one hand, vindicated. "There, that clinches it," she announced. Both men looked at her skeptically. There was something akin to pity in the M.E.'s eyes. She explained further, "Clancy was pathologically afraid of needles. A couple of years ago, he came down with something and was running a dangerously high fever. The doctor wanted to inject antibiotics to lower it and Clancy categorically refused. It wasn't until he passed out that the doctor managed to give him the shot." She looked at Mike. "Clancy was murdered."

He had just one question for her. "Why?"

Natalya blew out a breath, frustrated. If she knew why, she might know who. "I don't know, Detective. That's your job."

The M.E. shifted from one foot to another. Mike nodded at the man and the latter happily withdrew from what was gearing up to be the field of battle.

"What was his job?" Mike wanted to know. Maybe that had something to do with the way the man had wound up.

"He worked at a mortuary. Ellis Brothers." Except that the brothers had long since sold the business. The funeral parlor was now owned by a chain that in turn had hired Walter Tolliver to run it. "He was the one who brought the bodies in from the hospital." She raised her eyes to look at the closed door. A door Clancy was now behind. "Or the morgue." She saw Mike shaking his head. She couldn't make out his expression. "What?"

"I don't get it," he told her honestly.

"Don't get what?" she asked. "Why Clancy was murdered?"

"No, what you and he had in common. You're a bright, outgoing, intelligent, professional woman with a good practice and he was an irritating loser with a dead-end job and no friends. I don't see the connection."

For the first time, he saw anger enter her

eyes. It occurred to him that she could be a formidable force when stirred.

"Clancy wasn't a loser. People didn't get him. He was irritating because that was what he used as a defense mechanism. So many people made fun of him, he blocked them out, turned them away before they could say something hurtful. Under all that barbed wire was a funny, smart, warm person who just wanted to be liked." Even as she defended him, her heart ached because now Clancy would never find any happiness. Because now there were no more tomorrows for him.

Lowering her voice Natalya continued. "He wanted to be a doctor, you know, but he'd spent so much time skipping school—keeping away from bullies," she added before the detective could say something cryptic, "that he didn't have the grades to get into medical school."

He supposed, in some odd way, there was a connection between the two. "So he worked with dead bodies instead."

"It wasn't going to be permanent," she informed him tersely. Even dead, she was still defending him. "But he had bills to pay, so he took a job. He didn't like it, but it was a living. For the time being," she emphasized. She saw what looked like a smile descend over the detective's face. Was he laughing at her? At Clancy? "What?"

"He was lucky to have you." And he meant it. Few people had friends that would have stood by them the way she had.

"It wasn't just one-sided," she told him. "He would have done anything for me." Once he was certain that she wasn't going to tease him herself, Clancy couldn't do enough to show her his gratitude for their friendship. "Loyalty is a very rare thing, Detective. Clancy knew how to be loyal. And I wasn't his only friend," she added with feeling. "My family liked him."

He nodded. "The five doctors."

"And my parents," she added. Taking a breath, she braced her shoulders. Since she'd convinced him, in a manner, that Clancy had been murdered, maybe it was time to go home. For now. "When can I claim the body?"

"Not for at least another twenty-four hours. If we determined that it's a homicide—"

Obviously the battle wasn't quite won. "When," she corrected tersely.

"When," he allowed. "We might have to keep the body a little longer. In either case, I'll let you know. Now, why don't you go home and get some rest?" He took out his cell phone and flipped it open. "I'll get an officer to drive you."

She could only interpret that one way. "You're staying here?"

"No, but I didn't think you'd want to go home on the back of a motorcycle at this time of night." He'd have one of the officers bring his motorcycle to the station. "The temperature's dropped down," he pointed out. At fifty miles an hour, the cold air would sting.

She shook her head and smiled. It had to be one of the saddest smiles he'd ever seen. "I don't mind. Unless you'd rather not."

He had no idea why, but he couldn't think of anything else he would have wanted to do more.

In a gesture intended purely to be comforting rather than intimate, Mike slipped his arm around her shoulders.

"C'mon." He began to guide her down the long, darkened corridor to the elevator.

Natalya fell into step beside him, glad not to be alone at a time like this.

Chapter 5

The party for his one-year-old nephew wasn't until the late afternoon. That gave Mike a little leeway time-wise. Instead of sleeping in, the way he did on most Saturdays, he decided to do a little investigating into the case fate had pushed him into last night.

Whether or not Clancy Donovan's death could be ruled as accidental or a homicide was still up in the air but he supposed that it didn't hurt to cross all his *t*'s and dot a few *i*'s. At least he could tell that knockout of a doctor he'd looked into the matter the way he'd promised.

It also gave him a reason to give her a call. He was going to drop by Donovan's place of work and then swing by the man's apartment to nose around. That way, his conscience, professionally and otherwise, would be clear.

As he left his apartment, he thought about calling his partner to let him know what was up. He discarded the thought almost as soon as it occurred to him. This was the weekend. Louis used weekends to play catch-up at being the husband and father his wife wanted him to be. The guy had enough problems. There was no point in dragging him in for what could ultimately be ruled an accidental drug overdose despite what Clancy's very steadfast, very sexy friend maintained.

* * *

As a rule, Mike hated mortuaries, hated being anywhere near them. Mortuaries meant funerals. The only funerals he attended were for people who meant something to him, either personally, or symbolically, like a fellow officer. He didn't like thinking about death if he didn't have to.

Mike smiled cynically to himself as he pulled up in the parking lot behind Ellis Brothers Mortuary. The way he felt made the business he was in rather odd. But he was what he was and he was good at it. He liked to think that in the grand scheme of things he sometimes made a difference. He concentrated on the lives he saved by putting killers away. It was what kept him going.

Walter Tolliver had been brought in by the corporation that had bought the Ellis Brothers out several years ago. Tall, thin and courtly looking in an old-world sort of way, to the people who worked for him he was a tough, no-nonsense boss whose main concern was making money. He treated the bereaved with polite, sympathetic kindness, his employees with something a great deal less.

The rehearsed smile on the man's lips faded the moment Tolliver realized that he wasn't about to make a sale, but was being asked about Clancy. It was immediately apparent from his manner that Clancy had not been his favorite employee.

Eyes as gray as the suits he favored narrowed. "Clancy leaves a lot to be desired. As a matter of fact—" he tugged on his cuffs one at a time, utilizing a dramatic pause "—I'm thinking of letting him go."

"Why?" Mike asked mildly.

A cynical smile had found its way to the funeral director's lips. "Are you thinking of hiring him?"

Mike took out his badge and held it up. Nothing got his ire up faster than a smart mouth. "I'm thinking of getting some answers to my questions. Why would you let Mr. Donovan go?"

The sight of the badge caused Tolliver to sit back at his desk again. "Because he's late, he's rude and he's lazy. Now why are you asking?"

Mike studied him closely, wondering if Tolliver was just a garden variety pompous ass, or if there was more to him. "Because he was found dead last night."

"Oh." Tolliver took in a breath and then released it. He took in another before asking, "What happened?"

Not a bad performance, Mike mused. His

job had made him cynical way before his time he decided. "We're still piecing that together. What time did he leave here last night?"

Tolliver paused to think. "The usual time. As a matter of fact, I think he left a few minutes early. I was busy with the Wallace family at the time. Large family," he commented. Rocking back in his chair, Tolliver stroked his pencil-thin mustache. "I'm sorry to hear about Donovan," he finally said. "He wasn't a good worker, but still, to die so young…" A spark of interest entered his gray eyes. "Do you know if the family has made any arrangements yet?"

You are a piece of work, mister. Mike's voice was devoid of any emotion as he replied, "Not that I know of."

Tolliver nodded, as if he'd expected nothing less. "I'd be happy to make all the arrangements for them—at cost, of course."

Of course. "I'll pass it along. Thanks for your time," Mike mumbled as he walked out of his office. He couldn't get out of the oppressive building fast enough.

"Damn," Mike muttered, getting back onto his motorcycle. It hummed to life as he kicked away the stand. Expensive suits notwithstanding, the gray-haired, aristocratic-looking man was the closest thing to a vulture he'd encountered in quite a while.

His next stop was to see Clancy's mother.

Lucille Donovan looked as if she could have been very pretty once. But time and bitterness had left their imprint, like muddied boots across a neglected garden. She'd long since let herself go, except for a slash of lipstick too red for her coloring. The woman's mouth had a downward turn, making her appear to disapprove of everything she heard, everything she said.

At first, she didn't want to open the door, even after he'd shown her his badge.

"Any kid with half a brain can get one of those. Think I'm stupid?"

"No, Mrs. Donovan, I don't," he told her patiently. "I'm here about your son. Clancy," he said when she made no response.

"I know my son's name," Lucille snapped. She tugged up a bra strap that insisted on slipping from her shoulder. "What about him?"

The words never tasted any better. There was always the hint of bile in his mouth when he spoke them. "I'm sorry to have to be the one to tell you this, Mrs. Donovan, but your son was found dead last night."

The brown eyes widened instantly. "You shoot him? You kill my little boy?" Lucille demanded in a hysterical voice pumped with emotion that seemed to come out of nowhere.

"No, ma'am, I found him. We don't know what the cause of death was yet." It was a lie that he felt would buy him a little time. He watched as the woman's bravado receded. He guessed that, for a moment, she'd seen dollar signs in her head, hoping to sue the city for the wrongful death of her son. Now that there was no profit to be made, the hardened look was back.

"Well, I don't know what you're coming to me for. I can't afford to bury him." She threw up her hands, as if to push away any lingering hint of responsibility. "I'm a poor woman. You'll have to do whatever it is you do when you find those dead homeless people." Still standing in the doorway, her square, plump body, encased in a vivid red housedress, blocked any access into the house. Lucille looked over her shoulder as someone stirred in the background. She started to shut the door again. "Okay, you told me. Now go."

For now, he had no more questions, so he took his leave, walking down the cement steps back to the sidewalk. "You poor son of a bitch. I'm beginning to see why the doc felt so sorry for you," he said to himself.

He got back on his motorcycle and made a mental note to give his mother a kiss when he saw her. The woman was underappreciated.

It was becoming increasingly apparent to him that no one was going to miss Clancy except for the woman who had declared him missing in the first place.

Natalya.

In his mind's eye, he could visualize her face. Now there was someone he'd much rather be investigating than looking into the death of a man not even his mother seemed to like.

A traffic jam along Lexington nearly had him turning back. But just as he was about to turn down a side street, traffic began to trickle again, giving him enough of an opening to weave his bike in and out. It allowed him to make progress while cars of all sizes and shapes remained essentially hood to trunk. More than a couple of people cursed at him as he made his way to Clancy's apartment.

By the time he reached the fourth-floor walk-up, Mike was in less than a stellar mood. Parking had been another challenge. Both sides of the street were filled with not even enough space left over for a regular two-wheeler, much less his motorcycle. He was forced to double park. He had a right to do it while going about police business, but he still didn't like it.

The handwritten note on the superintendent's door said: Out.

It was turning out to be that kind of day, Mike thought, annoyed.

He went up to the apartment anyway. In a pinch, there were ways other than using keys to get into a place. Life on the street had taught him a few things even before he'd joined the force.

But he found that he didn't need to resort to an alternative method. The door to Clancy Donovan's apartment was already unlocked. The knob turned obligingly beneath his hand as he automatically checked it.

He laughed softly under his breath. "This character wasn't the brightest penny in the jar."

Despite popular classic sitcoms, you just

didn't leave your door unlocked in New York. It was begging for trouble.

Unless trouble was already here, he thought. His fingertips against the door, he pushed it open slowly. Just as he did, he thought he heard what sounded like a drawer being closed in the next room.

In less time than it took to think of it, he had his service revolver in his hands. Scanning the area, he inched his way into the small, pristine living room.

If the dead man owned a great many possessions, they were packed away somewhere else. Mike found himself looking at living quarters that were only a little more furnished than a Jesuit priest's cell.

White on white. Eerie, he thought.

The noise he'd heard had come from somewhere deeper in the apartment.

The next moment, Mike stepped on something that emitted a screeching wail. Every bone in his body tensed, braced for anything, as he moved back and looked down. There was a toy on the floor, the kind people bought for their pets. Even though he was no longer on it, the damn thing was still wailing. He resisted the urge to shoot it.

Standing in Clancy's miniscule kitchen, Natalya's head jerked up when she heard the high-pitched wail. Without thinking, she dropped the small digital camera she was about to look at into her coat pocket.

Someone was here. The killer?

Her heart pounding, she looked around for something to use as a weapon. She had just enough time to grab a chef's knife out of the wooden block when she heard someone call out, "Police. Come out with your hands up."

She released a sigh. She recognized that voice.

"How high up?" Natalya wanted to know, stepping out of the kitchen and into the living room. She had both hands raised shoulder level.

Mike swallowed a curse as he holstered his gun. He nodded at the weapon she was holding. "You can put the knife down."

Natalya looked at it as if she'd never seen it before. She hadn't realized she was still holding it. Relief that she wasn't going to be confronting Clancy's killer had temporarily turned her mind into a blank.

"Sorry." She took a step back into the kitchen and replaced the chef's knife where it belonged, then dusted off her hands as she joined Mike.

"What are you doing here?" he wanted to know.

He was studying her again. Why? Was he

back to thinking she had something to do with Clancy's death? "Looking for answers." He didn't look pleased. "I thought, since this wasn't a crime scene, it would be all right."

She didn't look as if she'd gotten too much sleep. Tired or not, she still looked a hell of a lot better than two-thirds of the female population. He reminded himself that he was a detective first, a red-blooded male second, but the position was hard to maintain.

"How do you know it's not the crime scene?"

She hated being put on the defensive. It wasn't a place where she was very comfortable. "Well, Clancy was found in the parking lot behind the gallery, so I just thought—" She stopped abruptly. "You're right, this could have been where whoever killed him injected Clancy with—what did you say it was?"

He hadn't said. But he did now. "Ketamin."

She could admit when she was wrong, he noted. Apparently she had a lot more going for her than killer legs.

Mike glanced down at the toy he'd stepped on. It was a god-awful turquoise color. He vaguely recalled reading that animals were color-blind. The choice, then, was to please the animal's owner. He stifled a shiver as he looked around the tiny apartment. "Your friend have a dog or cat?"

Natalya stooped down and picked up the toy. It was a cartoonish orangutan with extremely long arms. "Cat. Or at least he did. Thaddeus." Her mouth curved sadly. "I gave it to him. Thaddeus died three months ago. Someone poisoned him. Clancy had trouble getting over it."

Poisoned. A prank? he wondered. Or a warning?

For now, Mike kept the thought to himself. "Okay, then I don't have to keep looking over my shoulder, waiting to be bitten or scratched." He turned to look at her. "You have to go."

"I don't bite or scratch," she volunteered, then added. "Unless provoked."

The sadness had left her smile. It took him a moment to draw his eyes away. Longer to unclench his gut. "I'll keep that in mind. But this *might* be a crime scene and you've probably disturbed enough as it is."

"I watch all the crime shows, I was careful," she assured him. But he was right, this could be a crime scene. So, with a shrug, Natalya placed the incredibly blue orangutan on the sofa where Clancy had kept it after Thaddeus had been laid to rest. She raised her eyes to Mike's. The detective was watching her every move. The thought created a very warm shiver down her spine.

"You'll call me if you find something?"

"I'll call you," he promised.

Taking a deep breath, she nodded. "Okay." With that, she made her way to the door. But before she could open it and cross the threshold into the dank hallway, she heard the detective call out her name.

"Well, that was a little sooner than I expected." She looked at him over her shoulder, but he'd left the room. His voice sounded as if it was coming from the bedroom.

Retracing her steps, she found the detective standing before Clancy's closet. The expression on his handsome face was barely contained frustration. He had put on plastic gloves and one hand was wrapped around the doorknob. From the looks of it, he had tried to open the closet. And failed.

"The doors are locked," he told her.

She'd forgotten about that. "Clancy was a little paranoid," she told him. Then, in case he thought Clancy eccentric or crazy, she explained, "Happens after you deal with bullies a lot."

He nodded, only half hearing her. "Do you know where he kept the key?"

"No, but I know where I keep mine." Taking her purse off her shoulder, she pulled out a key.

Mild surprise crossed his features. "You have a key to his closet?"

"I told you I'd come in handy. Clancy wanted me to have a copy in case someone stole his."

A person with nothing to hide wouldn't lock their closet. "If he was into anything illegal, now would be the time to tell me."

"He was just into being Clancy, which meant that he was a little eccentric."

A little? "The woman has a gift for understatement. Who knew?" Mike muttered under his breath as he watched her unlock the doors.

Opening both doors for him, Natalya stepped back and let Mike deal with the walk-in closet. "I'm told I'm full of surprises."

He spared her a glance and made himself a promise that he was going to find out the nature of those surprises before more time passed.

And then he looked into the closet.

"Damn," he muttered.

Natalya looked around his shoulder, trying to see what he had. She didn't see anything out of the ordinary. "What?"

Every hanger pointed in the same direction. Shirts were grouped by length of sleeve and light to dark. The same for pants.

"Your friend was the daughter my mother always wanted. My sisters are both tornadoes," he confided. He looked into the closet again, still amazed. Most of his clothes were piled up on a chair where he'd shed them after a full day at work. Periodically he tossed the most wrinkled offenders into the wash. "This friend of yours was a neat freak."

Which, now that he thought of it, made him wonder about the fallen toy.

"He believed in that old adage: a place for everything and everything in its place."

Mike just nodded, still looking into the closet. "Makes things easier to find. If there's anything to find," he qualified. On one side, there were a handful of books on the shelf, arranged by size. He shook his head. Incredible.

She fervently hoped that there was something to find. Something that would make sense out of all this. She didn't want Clancy buried with a blot on his name. He *hadn't* overdosed, *hadn't* killed himself.

"Do you want me to stick around?" Natalya offered, raising her eyes to his face.

He detected the bit of smugness in her voice. He supposed he had it coming. And then he smiled. "Might as well," he told her. "There might be something else I can't open."

The look he gave her was so significant, it was hard for her not to look away. But she prided herself on facing every challenge. It was something Sasha had taught her by example.

"Sometimes just saying 'please' works wonders," she said.

Mike nodded. "Something else to keep in mind."

"You look terrible," Magda Pulaski declared the moment she saw her daughter walking into the small living room. Her three other sisters were already there. Only Sasha was missing.

On her feet instantly, Magda crossed to Natalya, determined to feel for a fever. For a thermometer she relied on the age-old tradition of placing her lips on her daughter's forehead. Natalya's forehead was cool, but Magda remained concerned and unsatisfied.

"When you working in the hospital, you can catch anything and more," she lamented.

Having indulged her mother, Natalya pulled her head back. Her temper felt short. "I didn't catch anything, Mama."

"She's too busy trying not to get caught," Marja, the youngest of the group, laughed. Everyone in the family knew that, until recently, Natalya did not lack for male attention. All her free time was spent socializing. But of late, she'd gone through a change. Her focus had shifted and she'd been spending more time at the hospital, more time at home.

Their father said Natalya had grown up. Their mother worried it might be something else.

Tania was about to raise her voice to add to the mix, but Magda held up her hand, signaling that the chatter was to cease. Her hazel eyes narrowed as she regarded Natalya, her mother's instincts telling her that something was wrong.

"What is it?" she wanted to know. "Why do you look as if someone had taken away your soul?"

"Maybe the girl does not want to talking, Magda," Josef protested, coming to his daughter's aid. He dearly loved his wife, but there were times when the woman did not know when to retreat.

Magda spared him a glance, then looked back at Natalya. "She wants to talk," she said firmly. Her eyes met Natalya's. "We are family, Natalya. We are here to help." She took her daughter's hands in hers, her expression softening. She could feel Natalya's pain. It all but radiated. "How can we help?"

Natalya pressed her lips together. She'd promised herself that she wasn't going to say anything, at least not today. Getting off the subway a block away from her parents' house and walking up to their door, she'd silently vowed that she wasn't going to ruin something her mother had been looking forward to for so long, ever since Sasha had been born. Sasha had called her late last night to tell her that she and Tony had decided to get married before Christmas. Mama had gotten on the phone and, in typical Mama style, had arranged everything. The wedding was in three weeks.

Today Natalya, her sisters and her mother were going to plan Sasha's bridal shower.

This was supposed to be a happy time. But

after she and the detective had left Clancy's apartment, going their separate ways, Natalya had suddenly felt this overwhelming sense of sorrow. Clancy was dead and no one cared. While he went through Clancy's apartment, Mike had mentioned that he'd stopped by Lucille Donovan's house to tell her that Clancy was gone and she'd protested that she had no money to bury him.

That statement was a crock because Clancy had told her his grandfather had died a couple of years ago, leaving a sizable amount of money to Lucille.

It wasn't right. It wasn't fair.

But she was supposed to have better control over herself than this. It just bothered her so that there was no one to mourn Clancy. And the kind look on her mother's face made it impossible for her to hold it in the way she wanted to.

The rest of the family gathered around her, closing ranks. Forming a protective ring around her. Something Clancy had never known.

It broke down the last of her reserve. "Clancy's dead, Mama."

Magda covered her mouth with her hand, her eyes darting toward her husband before returning to rest on her daughter's face.

"No," she cried in disbelief. "How? When? He was such a young person."

"What happened, Nat?" Kady pressed gently, her hand on Natalya's shoulder. Her festive, teasing manner abruptly vanished in the wake of this news. Although Natalya and Sasha were closer in age—only eleven months apart—she and Kady were closer in spirit. Growing up, they'd formed a bond. Allies in a large family were always welcomed.

Natalya took a breath, silently blessing them

all for being there. "The police think it's a drug overdose."

"But you do not," Josef assumed. It wasn't a question.

"Clancy did not take drugs," Magda reminded him with authority that God would have trouble arguing with.

"What do you think happened?" Kady asked her.

Natalya blew out a breath. "What I think is that Clancy was murdered."

The last word hung there in the air for a moment. And then her father said a word in Polish that neither he nor his wife had ever taught them. For once, Magda didn't upbraid him. She merely nodded her head as sorrow gathered in her eyes.

Chapter 6

The house was fairly packed with family and more than a few friends. At the center of it were the children, laughing, playing, chasing each other around while their parents tried to carry on some semblance of a coherent conversation. Gentle admonishments were liberally sprinkled within almost every other sentence.

It was a typical DiPalma party.

Josephine DiPalma, a petite woman who

still had almost midnight-black hair except for one prominent silver streak just at her right temple, worked her way through the crowd and presented her second son with an oversized piece of cake.

To the amusement of his parents, Sofia and her husband, Jake, the guest of honor had just christened his nose with whipped chocolate frosting by bobbing his face into the plate on his high-chair tray. Alan was wearing his birthday cake and loving it.

"Does this give you any ideas?" Josephine asked, pushing the plate into his hands.

After one of his mother's typical six-course meals, there was no room left over for a spoonful of gelatin, much less a piece of cake, but he accepted the plate, knowing that if he didn't her feelings would be hurt. She'd baked the cake, too.

Even so, it was obvious that his mother wasn't referring to the cake. Mike laughed and kissed her on the forehead just beneath her widow's peak.

"You're a great many things, Ma," he told her affectionately, "but subtle isn't one of them."

Josephine sniffed, settling in beside her son. There was almost a foot difference.

"I wasn't trying to be subtle, I was trying to become a grandmother again—in the proper order," she emphasized before Mike could give her that wicked wink that'd had females of all ages melting around him since her son had reached puberty. "First marriage, then baby."

He wouldn't have had it any other way. But for the moment, he was in no hurry for either. His present lifestyle suited him just fine.

"'Fraid you've got a long wait then, Ma.

Why don't you just enjoy what you have?" He nodded toward his sister, who was blossoming with her third child. Her first go-round had resulted in twins. For Theresa's sake, he hoped she wouldn't be overwhelmed again. "Aren't you the one who always tells me to count my blessings?"

Josephine was not about to be distracted. "One of those blessings should be a wife."

He tried to look at his mother as solemnly as possible, but the slight curve at the corner of his mouth gave him away. "Sorry, Ma, but you've spoiled me for any other woman."

The dismissive snort told him that his mother wasn't buying any of this. "The problem is that in your line of work you don't meet any nice girls, Michael. They're either harlots or dead."

Mike choked on his cake. From out of

nowhere, his mother produced a glass of wine. Mike took a long drink, clearing his throat. "Nobody says harlots anymore, Ma."

"Your mother does," his father said, his voice mild as he came up behind them. He draped one still-muscular arm—a trophy of fifty years as a skilled tile layer—along his son's shoulders. His father turned his face toward him. "Need rescuing?"

Mike glanced toward his mother before answering. He had genuine affection for her. For both his parents. But he wished that she could be content weaving in and out of his siblings' lives. Carl wasn't married, but he was engaged and it was beginning to look serious for Matt and his girl. Theresa was working on her third child and Sofia had Alan. Only he and Claudia were unattached and he had a feeling she might be capitulating soon.

"I need someone to change the topic," he told his father.

Salvatore pretended to frown. "Are you trying to marry him off again?" He wasn't fooling anyone. Everyone who knew the couple knew that, as far as Sal was concerned, nothing his wife said or did ever merited censure. Married on his twenty-first birthday, thirty-three years later he still doted on her.

Josephine didn't answer her husband's question. Instead, she looked at her son and sighed deeply. "Well, someone has to be concerned about him. Look at him." She gestured at him with both hands. "Thirty years old and no prospects. What kind of an Italian boy is that?" she demanded.

"A smart one." Sal chuckled. The remark had been aimed at Mike. Looking now at his wife, he pretended to be properly sobered. "Just kidding, Josie."

Curious, Carl had come up to join the small circle and had been privy to his mother's last question.

"Mike's got plenty of prospects, Ma." He rolled his eyes comically, a wistful expression on his brutally handsome face. He clapped his brother's back. They were almost the same height, with Mike less than an inch taller. "I should have prospects like Mikey, here."

This time Josephine's frown was genuine. She wanted the best for all her children. Health, happiness and most of all, someone to love who loved them back. "One-day stands don't count."

"'Night,' Ma, one-night stands," Mike corrected her. His own words echoed back to him and he deftly backtracked. "And who says I've got one-night stands?" His expression was the epitome of innocence. All except the twinkle in his eyes. "I'm an altar boy, remember?"

That was too much for Carl. "A funny thing happened on your way to the altar," he cracked. "You became a playboy."

"My job leaves me too tired for that kind of stuff," Mike responded, giving his brother a warning look. Josephine DiPalma was a sharp woman. He had a hunch that she knew a great deal more about the kind of life he led than she was saying, but he didn't want to be blatant about it. For the most part, it was a game they both played and he for one was content to leave it at that for now.

And then his mother surprised him. "Bull."

Mike's jaw dropped open, as did the jaws of all the DiPalma men. Josephine DiPalma didn't talk that way. "Ma."

Josephine jabbed her forefinger at Mike's

chest. "You heard me. Ever since you broke up with Brenda, you just go from woman to woman."

That wasn't strictly true. For the most part, he didn't have the time to be the Romeo Carl was making him out to be. But every encounter he *did* have had been superficial by design. Mike focused on the one saving point his mother seemed to have forgotten. "You didn't like Brenda, remember?"

Josephine waved her hand dismissively. "Beside the point. I would have turned her into a proper DiPalma woman."

Mike inclined his head toward his brother and said in a stage whisper, "Remind me to send Brenda a note telling her that I saved her."

His mother's arched eyebrows narrowed dangerously. "Laugh."

Mike held his hands up before him in a visible protest. "Wouldn't dream of it."

Josephine took his face between her hands the way she had when he was a little boy. Except that now she had to stand on her toes to do it. "I just don't want you to wind up old and alone, Michael."

Gently he removed her hands and for a second held them in his. "With all the nieces and nephews everyone else is going to be giving me because you've given them quotas to fill, I might wind up old, but alone is the last thing I'll ever be."

She refused to be amused. For the moment, she blocked out the rest of her family, trying to convert the unconverted. "I'm serious, Michael."

"Uh-oh," Matt murmured as he came to see what this impromptu family meeting was about. "Ma's using your full first name. If she throws in the middle one, I'd say it was time to run."

For a moment, Josephine relented. She retreated to the one person who never gave her any grief or opposition. Standing with her back against him, she took both his hands and wrapped them around her waist as she looked at three of her sons. "I just want everyone to be as happy as your father and I are."

Maybe that was part of the problem, Mike thought. His parents were a tough act to follow, much less live up to. "Not possible, Ma."

Josephine nodded toward the youngest of the DiPalma men. "Why can't you bring me a nice girl like your brother Matt?"

Mike laughed. "There aren't any nice girls like Matt and a good thing, too. They'd be ugly enough to stop a clock." He saw the exasperated look his mother gave him. He knew that look. It meant that he'd pushed her as far as she was willing to go. "Okay, okay, I promise. The next time I'm in the store, I'll go down the nice girl aisle and pick one out." He leaned down, bringing his face next to his mother's. He gave her a quick kiss on the cheek. "Until then, enjoy the party. Remember, a kid only turns one once." With that, he retreated before his mother could gear up for another round.

He liked going over to see his family. He liked coming home to the peace and quiet of his apartment just as much. He loved his parents dearly but the moment he'd turned twenty-one, the age his father had married his mother, his mother started to drop hints. Initially they'd descended on him a drop at a time. At thirty, they were coming down with the intensity of a storm at sea.

Tonight, she'd been in rare form. Eventually, to gain a little peace, he'd told her that he was actually seeing someone. His mother's face had lit up and then turned suspicious as she'd asked where this so-called "someone" was. He'd placated his mother by saying that she'd had a prior engagement, making the commitment before he'd asked her to Alan's party. Then, before his mother could say anything, he quickly tacked on that she was shy, so he wasn't certain when a meeting would come up.

It surprised him a little that the woman he'd summoned to mind when giving his mother the most cursory of answers had been the doctor he'd met yesterday. Natalya.

Funny how she'd managed to stick in his head like that.

But then, when a woman looked the way

Natalya Pulaski did, if she hadn't stuck in his mind he would have seriously had himself checked over for a pulse.

So now he was stuck with a fictitious romance his mother was sure to ask about. He glanced at the phone. He had to admit he was surprised that it wasn't ringing, that his mother wasn't calling for more substantial details. He could only hope that the others would keep her busy.

Two weeks. He was going to give the "romance" two weeks and then tell his mother that they broke up. She'd respect his space for a while, giving him sympathy and sending his brothers over with food, the way she had when he'd stopped seeing Brenda. With any luck, it would buy him a reprieve for about a month or so.

Emptying his pockets, Mike tossed his wallet

and keys onto the coffee table. A somewhat crushed card was peering out of his wallet.

Her card, he thought as he picked it up. She'd given it to him so that he could call if there were any new developments. For a second, he just held the card, debating. And then he shrugged. What the hell? One way or the other, there was nothing to lose.

Going with impulse, something he placed a fair amount of faith in, Mike dialed the cell phone number Natalya'd written on the back of her card.

He counted off five rings and was about to hang up when she picked up. "Hello?"

Her voice sounded low, sexy, moving in waves over the phone. "Doc?"

He could almost hear her snapping to attention. Belatedly, he realized what she probably thought. "Did you find anything?"

Feeling a little guilty he replied, "No. I was just wondering if you were up for a cup of coffee, or a nightcap." When there was no response, a smattering of awkwardness seeped in. It was an entirely new sensation for him and it took effort to shut it down. "Never mind, bad idea."

"No." The single word crackled as it shot out of her mouth. "Not a bad idea." The volume of her voice lowered again. "A good idea." She hesitated a moment, as if undecided whether or not to admit something. "I was actually thinking about calling you."

Maybe this wasn't a mistake after all. "Oh?"

"Yes, I just remembered a piece of information that might be able to help you."

A vague disappointment stirred through him. This wasn't what he'd expected her to say. "Oh."

If Natalya didn't know better, she would have said that was disappointment in his voice.

Probably her hearing playing tricks on her. She really wasn't sure of anything anymore. Ever since they'd discovered Clancy's body, everything felt as if it had been turned on its ear.

"Where do you want me to meet you?" she asked.

He didn't want her standing on some corner, waiting. "I'll pick you up," he told her. "Do you need to get ready?"

"Excuse me?"

He didn't mean to imply that she should do something special, but he was accustomed to his sisters' behavior. "My sisters always needed time to get ready. Whenever they had to go anywhere, they spent an average of forty-five minutes in the bathroom first, with hair dryers, makeup and an armload of clothes."

Her laugh was almost musical. "I just got in. I'm ready now."

"Just got in," he echoed. Mike picked up his helmet on his way out the door. "Had an emergency?" It seemed a logical assumption, given her profession.

Was that his way of feeling her out to find out if she'd come back early from a date? No, she was giving this too much weight, Natalya upbraided herself.

But then what kind of weight should she be attaching to this invitation that had come out of the blue?

Not into playing games, she gave him an honest answer. "My family is many things, but I never quite thought of them as an emergency."

Talk about a small world. "You went to see your family?"

She couldn't quite make out his tone. Was it amusement? "Yes, why?"

Mike shifted his phone from one hand to the

other, suspending his helmet strap around his wrist as he slid his jacket back on. "Nothing. It's just that I just came home from seeing mine."

That would explain the amusement. "We have something in common."

Natalya sank into the deep cushion of the sofa she and Sasha had picked out together when they'd first began to furnish the apartment. She tucked her legs beneath her seat.

"I guess we do," she heard him say. "Your mother nag you about being single?"

In response to his question, Mike was rewarded with a rich laugh. The sound spread through his veins like warm honey mixed with brandy as he made his way down the stairwell.

"Every so often. With Sasha getting married," she confided, "the pressure's off a little."

He could relate to that. "Yeah, I know what you mean." He'd reached the ground floor and pushed the door open. His bike was parked close to his building. "I'm going to need both my hands now."

He did throw things at her out of left field. "Excuse me?"

"My motorcycle." He got astride it as he explained. "It requires two hands. I never got a Bluetooth attachment. Don't like anything hanging on my ear," he told her before she could ask. "I've got to hang up. See you in ten."

Ten minutes? Natalya sat up. "Just how close are you to my apartment?" she wanted to know. But she was asking the dial tone. Mike had terminated the connection.

Flipping her phone closed, Natalya got up off the sofa. She glanced toward the bathroom. Maybe a once-over wasn't such a bad idea.

If he was right, there were only nine and a half minutes left.

* * *

He wound up taking her to a coffee shop located a few blocks from the apartment she shared with her sisters. Expecting it to be packed, she was pleasantly surprised to find the Saturday night crowd had thinned out.

Mike steered her toward a table with a view of the sidewalk, but away from the door and the draft that was created when it was opened.

Setting down the small tray he was holding, he took a seat and looked at Natalya. Most of the tables were for two, which allowed them to create an illusion of intimacy within the surrounding din of noise and moving bodies.

As she sat down, their knees touched. The wave of attraction that had been filtering between them intensified.

Taking their oversized cups from the tray, he slipped it under the table, balancing it on its edge against the central table leg so that they had more room.

It was time to get what was on her mind out of the way so that whatever it was that was humming between them could have room to flourish.

"All right," Mike began genially, "so what was it that you suddenly remembered and were going to call me about when I beat you to the punch?"

She'd had time to roll it over in her head. When she did, it had sounded a bit melodramatic, but then it had come from Clancy and Clancy had a tendency toward drama. And it could mean something. No stone unturned, she told herself.

Natalya leaned forward so he could hear her without her having to raise her voice. "A few weeks ago Clancy began hinting that he was on to something underhanded going on at the mortuary."

"Underhanded," Mike repeated. She nodded. "Did he tell you what?"

This time, Natalya shook her head. "I asked him but he wouldn't go into detail. Which was strange for Clancy," she admitted. "He said that he wanted to be sure first before he told me anything else." She could see that she was losing him. She was quick to add, "But he made it sound as if he thought it was big." A sliver of guilt pricked at her now. She should have pressed Clancy, made him elaborate. "I thought that he was just imagining things because he didn't like the funeral director and this was a way of putting himself in a more favorable light."

For a second, she paused, wrestling with a feeling of disloyalty. But she had to tell the detective everything so that he had the whole picture. "Clancy had a tendency to be a little melodramatic at times." She sighed, wrapping her long fingers around the cup, absorbing its warmth. "I didn't pay attention, but maybe if I had, he'd be alive now."

He didn't want her blaming herself. Nothing useful came of it. "You can't know that."

Oh, but she could. She did. Natalya raised her eyes to his. "Ever have a feeling, Detective? Something deep in your gut that tells you something even though your common sense says something else?"

He looked at her for a long moment. So long that it took her breath away. "Sometimes," he allowed.

It took her a second to draw air back into her lungs. She focused hard on what she was saying, nearly losing the thread. He'd made her mind go momentarily blank, taking her somewhere that had nothing to do with what she was trying to say.

"That's how I feel about this," she finally continued. "Clancy's death is because of something that's going on at the mortuary."

Chapter 7

"Such as?" Mike pressed when Natalya didn't elaborate on her statement.

With a frustrated sigh, Natalya was forced to shrug helplessly, a condition she had little use for and absolutely hated. As far back as her memory would take her, she'd always been a doer, someone who struck immediately, quickly, taking care of whatever needed doing. Despite her outwardly carefree attitude, she liked to burrow into the heart of a problem and work her way out, learning and solving as she went.

But here, when it involved someone she cared about, she was at a loss.

"I don't know," she finally admitted ruefully, holding the container in both hands and moving it absently back and forth between her palms. And then she began to theorize. Her eyes became a little brighter as she talked. "Ellis Brothers isn't that far from Our Lady of Patience Memorial Hospital. We send them our John and Jane Does, people the city ambulance brings us who don't make it and haven't been identified. Clancy told me that the mortuary has a contract with the city and handles the burials. Sometimes he'd be the one to come and pick up the bodies."

He'd pop in, first in the pediatric wing, then, if she wasn't there, in her office across the street. He always looked so happy to see her.

She was never going to see that bright, smiling face again, she realized for the dozenth time. Natalya banked down the wave of sadness that came a beat after that first thought.

It was getting a little noisier. A crowd of six entered the small shop. Mike leaned forward. "Where's this headed?"

Natalya wasn't sure just yet. She continued using him as a sounding board. "Maybe there were some irregularities—the mortuary over-charging the city, charging for handling bodies that ultimately were identified on their premises but whose funerals weren't handled by the mortuary. Or maybe the mortuary was even charging for handling bodies that didn't exist."

It struck her as a viable theory. Maybe, if Clancy had stumbled across it, he'd been killed to keep him from talking.

Oh, God, Clancy, why couldn't you have just

left well enough alone? Or told a cop? If she knew Clancy, he would have gone to Tolliver and told him he was exposing him just for the satisfaction of seeing horror on the man's face.

The more she thought about it, the more she was sure she was on the right track. "You've got people who could look into that, right? Computer experts."

She looked so eager, so intent on helping, that Mike caught himself suppressing a smile. "Yes—"

"Because if you don't," she continued, the tempo of her voice rising as the flow of words from her lips became faster, "Kady is dating an accountant who knows someone that used to work at the IRS and she could ask him to look—"

"Kady?" Mike repeated the name, stopping her in midflight.

"Leokadia." She gave him her sister's full name, even though no one, not even her parents, called her that. "My younger sister. Or one of them," she clarified, since there were three. "We call her Kady because it's a lot easier on everyone's tongue."

He'd never heard the name before. But then, with so many different nationalities coming into New York every year, that was becoming more of the norm. "Yeah, I'd imagine it would be."

Natalya fell back into her narrative. "Anyway, Kady could ask Henry if—"

He had to stop her before she literally ran him over with her rhetoric. "No need to ask Henry anything." Whoever Henry was, he thought. "We'll handle it from here."

She took a breath. Did that mean he was convinced this was a homicide and that the blame lay with the mortuary? "Good."

Given what he'd seen of her take-charge nature, he hadn't expected her to surrender so easily. He proceeded with caution, feeling his way around.

"Glad you approve." His eyes slid over her face. No doubt about it, the more he looked at her, the more beautiful she seemed to become. How was that possible? He decided to take the next viable step forward. Caution on a case was something he was accustomed to. Caution with a woman was something else. Something new. "So listen, are you in the mood for dinner or something—"

Her pager went off before he had a chance to finish his question. It was clipped to her belt and she immediately glanced at it. Her answering service number pulsed in bright blue relief.

More than a tinge of disappointment

slipped over her, surprising her by its unexpected appearance.

"Looks like we might have to shelve 'dinner or something,'" she murmured. Taking out her cell phone, Natalya called her service. A short exchange of words had her jotting down the home number of one of her patients.

He waited until she terminated the call. "Do you have to leave?"

Natalya shook her head. "Don't know yet." She tapped out the number the service had given her. The phone was answered on the first ring. Mike could hear the tone of the voice on the other end of the line. It sounded distraught. Whoever it was was sobbing.

"Slow down, Mrs. Cummings," Natalya told the woman, her own voice deadly calm. "Now, what did you say were the symptoms?"

Mike sat back and observed Natalya. Her

exuberant tone had gone down several notches as she said what she could to calm whoever was on the other end of the line.

She was pretty good under fire, he thought. He liked a woman who could think on her feet and who could change gears so quickly. Only seconds ago, she'd sounded so impassioned when she was talking to him about her friend and why she thought he'd wound up being killed.

"Bundle Stacey up and bring her over to Patience Memorial. I'll meet you in the emergency room in twenty minutes. No, she's not going to die, Mrs. Cummings, I give you my word," she assured her with feeling. "I know. These things can be scary. Right. Twenty minutes." Ending the call, Natalya closed her phone with both hands, as if she were applauding. And then she looked at him. There was genuine regret on her face. "I have to go."

He nodded as she tucked her cell phone away. "I heard."

She hadn't fully realized how much she wanted to spend time with this man until the opportunity was taken away from her. "Sorry."

"Hey, part of the job." His mouth curved a little. She found it incredibly appealing. "I know all about having to dash away from something because of a phone call." Mike rose to his feet.

Natalya glanced at his cup. He hadn't finished his coffee. "You don't have to leave on my account."

The smile widened. "It was kind of on your account that I was here to begin with," he reminded her. "C'mon, I'll take you to the hospital."

She didn't want him to be put out. "You don't have to. I can catch a cab."

But Mike had already gently taken hold of her arm and was now guiding her toward the door. Another wave of people had come in and there was now a line to the counter. "My father always told us to leave with the girl you brought."

She moved before him as he held the door open for her. The sudden shift of cold air was a bracing surprise. "I think that refers to going to a party."

He looked down at Natalya for a second. "You mean this wasn't a party?"

She opened her mouth to make a disclaimer, then shut it again. Her lips formed a smile. She had no idea what "this" actually was.

Maybe "this" was just a nice interlude. Or maybe it was the beginning of something nicer. She couldn't tell. She also had no idea if she wanted it to be the beginning of something more serious.

But there was definitely something about the detective that was unraveling her, something that made her understand why moths flew into flames even though, somewhere along the line, they had to know it was inherently bad for them. The attraction was there. For both her and the moth.

She forced herself to focus on what was really important. The small patient on her way to the E.R. with her parents. "We'd better hurry. I told Mrs. Cummings twenty minutes."

"I heard," he acknowledged, amused.

She mounted the motorcycle behind him, her arms going around his waist. He allowed himself a half second to savor the feeling that flashed through him and then he took to the road.

They made it there in under fifteen minutes. Her cheeks were stinging and her fingers felt icy from hanging on to his waist. The night was crisp and clear and the wind was cold this time of night. The smell of November was definitely in the air.

As she got off the motorcycle, Natalya slid the helmet from her head and handed it to him. "Well, thanks again." She expected him to say something pleasant and rev the engine up a notch before disappearing into the night. Instead, he got off and locked the helmets into the saddlebag. She stared at him in minor confusion, aware that the parking valet to her right was staring at the bike with unabashed adulation. "You're coming with me?"

Mike nodded. "I'm always open to learning about things."

She looked at him skeptically, trying to interpret his comment. "You've never been to a hospital before?" It was more of a semimocking statement than a question.

The city had more than a handful of hospitals and at times it felt as if he'd been to most of them. But Patience Memorial had not numbered among them. He glanced up at the back of the edifice. "Not this one." And then he looked at the woman he'd escorted here. "Not with a personalized tour."

"We're going to have to put that tour on hold." Turning on her heel, she went through the electronic doors into the back of the E.R. There was no time to argue. From the sound of it, the baby did need medical attention and soon. If she didn't receive it, then quite possibly Stacey Cummings *would* be in the danger zone.

Natalya checked in at the outpatient reception desk just seconds ahead of the anxious couple and their crying eighteen-month-old. A quick examination showed that the baby was suffering from the croup, something that, Natalya assured Stacey's parents, was not fatal, but needed to be treated properly.

"Then we can take her home?" Mrs. Cummings asked eagerly.

"No, I'm afraid she needs to spend some time in an oxygen tent. Her lungs need to be cleared. We'll keep her here overnight for observation to be on the safe side and you can pick her up in the morning."

"She's never been away from home," Mrs. Cummings cried.

"No sleepovers yet?" Natalya teased gently. She put a comforting arm around the woman's shoulders. "We can arrange to have a cot, or two," she added, looking at Stacey's father, "put into the room so you can stay with her."

Mr. Cummings looked a little sheepish. "I just want a good night's sleep."

"One cot it is," Natalya agreed, ending any debate that might have begun between the parents. "The nurses actually prefer it that way." They really preferred no parents on the premises, but one was better than two, Natalya thought. "Let me make the arrangements."

It took approximately a half hour to make it all happen. Stacey and her mother were taken to the pediatric ward while an exhausted Mr. Cummings made his way out of the E.R., promising his wife to be back in the morning.

"That wasn't so bad, I guess," Natalya commented, signing the admission chart before surrendering it to the attending nurse.

The comment was directed to Mike, who had remained in the background throughout the exam and subsequent interaction between Natalya and the baby's parents. Now that it was over, he came forward. "You're pretty good under fire," he commented.

Natalya turned to face him. She caught the appreciative look the nurse gave him before retreating with the signed chart. Not that she blamed the woman, Natalya thought.

She hadn't forgotten about Mike, not for a moment. Which was highly unusual for her because, when she worked, her patients became the focus of her entire attention. There was nothing to spare, nothing left over. This time, she kept glancing over toward the man who stood against the wall, quietly observing her. Even as she examined the child, assessing her condition, she couldn't help wonder what was going on in the detective's mind. It annoyed her that her thoughts could stray like that, but at the same time, she had to admit that it did intrigue her. Because this was not business as usual for her.

"That was nothing. You should see me with triplets," she quipped.

She felt tired, but oddly wired at the same time. The wired feeling had nothing to do with hitting upon a correct, elusive diagnosis or making a tiny patient feel better though. This time, it had everything to do with the man who had happened into her life completely by accident. A man who shouldn't even have been there.

"Sounds interesting." Mike's tone matched her own. "Ready to leave?"

She'd signed her small patient in and there was nothing left to do for the night. Natalya nodded. "Ready."

They stood a few feet away from the reception desk. He looked at her for a long moment, feeling something stir, telling himself it was nothing more than the usual thrill of the hunt. Too bad it would recede the moment the hunt was a thing of the past. He liked this feeling, liked the exhilaration he felt surging through his veins. He savored it a moment longer, wishing there was a way to make it last.

But nothing ever lasted.

"Me, too," he replied quietly as he slipped his arm around her shoulders. Drawing her closer to him, he guided her out the rear E.R. doors that led out to the small parking lot.

His bike was exactly where he'd left it, against the far wall. The same valet who'd been there earlier was now standing beside it, eyeing it enviously.

"She's a beauty," the valet said, stepping back.

Mike slanted a glance toward Natalya. "Yes," he agreed. "She is."

For the first time in her life, Natalya felt a blush working its way up to the roots of her hair. She pretended not to make anything of the exchange. Instead, she took the helmet he handed her.

His cell phone began to ring just as she was about to mount the bike.

She left the chin strap unfastened. "Your turn." She nodded at the sound coming from the front pocket of his jeans.

God, he hoped not, Mike thought. Leaving his own helmet perched on the seat of the motorcycle, he pulled out his cell.

Any hope he'd been nurturing died the moment he said hello and heard Louis's voice on the other end. "We got a body, partner."

It was on the tip of his tongue to ask Louis to go solo on this case, at least for now. But Louis wouldn't have called unless both their presences were required by the captain. Besides, this was his job, and it had always come first before any thoughts of temporary pleasure.

He tried to console himself with the thought that the longer the end of the hunt was put off, the longer the thrill of pursuit, of the unknown, would continue. Somehow, it seemed a cold consolation.

Phone to his ear, he half turned, creating a pocket of space for himself. "Where?"

"Central Park."

The city had grown a great deal safer than it had been in the seventies and eighties, but there was still such a thing as common sense. Going into the park after dark was still not the smartest thing to do. But people seemed to check their brains at the entrance. It never ceased to amaze him.

"Jogger?" he guessed. The wind shifted and he could have sworn he caught a whiff of vanilla. He turned slightly toward Natalya. Her perfume? Shampoo? Or just his imagination?

"Homeless guy," Louis said. "He was stabbed several times, robbery obviously not the motive from the way he's dressed. I've started without you," Louis volunteered, then quipped, "but you know that it's never any fun when I'm by myself."

Mike bit off a sigh. There was no way around this. "All right. I'll be there as soon as I can."

"Sooner would be nice," Louis told him. There was shouting in the background and Louis swore under his breath.

"Yeah." Mike closed his phone, terminating the call. Regret nudged at him as he looked in Natalya's direction. "Looks like I'm going to have to take you home."

He'd come with her to her emergency, but she had a feeling that there wasn't going to be any reciprocation. "I take it this isn't a bring-your-date-to-the-office kind of thing."

Mike felt his mouth curving almost on its own. She'd referred to herself as his date. Normally, he didn't really like putting labels on things in his private life, but it didn't bother him this time. Maybe it was the humor in her eyes, or the need he felt in his gut, he wasn't sure, but something was definitely different here.

Or maybe that was because it'd been awhile since he'd been with anyone who remotely resembled a female without also being in the process of either questioning her, booking her or making notes before she was taken off to the morgue.

"Nope, I'm afraid not this time." He fastened her chin strap for her. "I'll take you home."

She put her hand over his, stopping him. Or maybe just wanting to touch him. "I can still get a cab," she reminded him.

He knew he should be on his way, grateful that she was being so understanding. But he wanted to bring her home. "This is faster, and I'd feel better knowing I brought you to your door."

A smile played on her lips. One that seemed to find its way straight to his gut. "Wouldn't want to get in the way of you feeling better," she told him. With that, she got on behind him, secured her arms around his waist and leaned in close. "Home, James."

Mike laughed as he kicked away the kickstand.

He'd meant just to leave her at the entrance to her building. The wind had picked up, making it even chillier than it already was, and he had a crime scene that was getting colder by the minute. But as Natalya slid off the back of his motorcycle, he could still feel the warmth of her body as she'd had it pressed against his. Instead of taking off, Mike found himself getting off the motorcycle, as well.

She took the gesture as one related to his previous claim to chivalry. "You *really* don't have to bring me upstairs to my door," she assured him. Amusement curved the edges of her lips, making them even more tempting than they already were.

"No," he agreed, "I've got to get going." But even as he said it, he made no move to get back on his bike. No move to leave her side.

"You're not going," she pointed out quietly. Nor did she want him to go, she realized, not entirely comfortable with the thought.

"No, I guess I'm not."

Mike struggled for a moment, wanting to kiss her, feeling that, given the circumstances, it might still be inappropriate.

And then, he looked into her eyes and the argument was settled.

He brought his mouth down to hers ever so fleetingly. At least, that was the initial intent. But the best laid plans of mice and men and off-duty police detectives did not always play out as plotted. Drawing her closer into his arms, Mike deepened the kiss just enough to turn it from friendly into something more.

How much more, he wasn't destined to find out just at that point. The middle of a street, even if it wasn't crowded, wasn't the place for this and he knew it. But it wasn't until his cell phone rang again that actual contact was broken.

Damn technology, he thought, struggling to keep his frustration in check. He yanked out the cell phone, snapping it open and pressing it to his ear.

"Hello?" he managed, just pulling himself out of what was the beginning of a tailspin.

"You coming or what?"

Louis. The terms of justifiable homicide flashed through his head.

"I'm coming, Louis," he bit off, then terminated the connection. He looked at Natalya. The outline of her lips was blurred. Seeing that excited him. "I've got to go."

"I heard." Which, considering how hard her heart was pounding, was nothing short of a minor miracle, Natalya thought.

Chapter 8

Natalya shed her lab coat and hung it on the back of her door, then sat down at her desk for a moment before leaving the office for the night.

The restless feeling that had been steadily growing all day was only getting worse. She took a breath, then slowly let it out. As she did so, she told herself to take it light.

She hadn't heard from Detective DiPalma in several days.

Four to be exact. And, despite the fact that her Monday had begun with a full complement of small patients all requiring her undivided attention, she grew progressively antsier as the day made its way into night. Tuesday was no better. By Wednesday—today—her nerves felt stretched to the limit.

Get a grip, Nat.

Better that she should concentrate on more important things, she reminded herself, and looked at the phone on her desk. An example being, why hadn't the morgue released Clancy's body yet? Had they found something more? Or was this an annoying matter of getting lost in the shuffle? Had someone just forgotten to call her to let her know she could pick up Clancy's remains? She didn't want to make a pest of herself, but she did have a mortuary in Queens on standby. Clancy deserved a proper funeral.

Calling the morgue wouldn't hurt anything, she silently insisted.

Just as her hand covered the black receiver, the phone rang beneath her palm. She debated letting her service answer it, then decided that the service would only call her and she in turn would only wind up calling back whoever was on the phone now.

Might as well eliminate the middle man.

She placed the receiver against her ear. "This is Dr. Pulaski."

"Right." The person on the other end seemed a little flustered, as if searching for the right words. "This is the coroner's office. We just wanted to let you know that Mr. Donovan's body has been released."

Talk about coincidence, she thought. Now she could finally put Clancy to rest. "I'll call the funeral parlor right away. They'll be there to pick him up within the hour." She refused to refer to Clancy's body, lifeless or not, as "it."

There was another pause on the other end. When he spoke, the man who'd called her sounded just the slightest bit confused. "They already came."

She didn't understand. What was he talking about? "Who came?"

"The guys from the funeral parlor." There was a touch of exasperation in the man's otherwise high-pitched voice. "I'm just calling because I happened to see your name on this paperwork, saying you wanted to be notified when we were through with the autopsy reports. I asked around but nobody called you."

"No, nobody called me." Natalya struggled to hang on to her temper. "What 'guys' from the funeral parlor?" she demanded. "And what funeral parlor?" To her best recollection, she hadn't notified the coroner's office as to which mortuary she wanted Clancy's remains sent to. Had the mortuary gotten in touch with the morgue for some reason? It didn't seem likely. But then, this man was telling her that Clancy's body had been claimed. Was this some mistake? Had they taken Clancy's body instead of someone else's?

"Wait a sec." As she listened impatiently, she heard paper being rustled on the other end. "Yes, here it is. Ellis Brothers. Ellis Brothers Mortuary. They sent the hearse." He cleared his throat a bit nervously. "I didn't sign for the transport personally, but—"

She didn't need to hear any more. "Thank you." Natalya hung up, incensed. The receiver almost bounced out of the cradle.

What the hell was going on here? Was this

some cruel joke on Tolliver's part? Or was the man just feeling remorseful over the way he'd treated Clancy?

Somehow, she doubted it, not after all the things that Clancy had told her about the director. Tolliver didn't seem like the remorseful type. If anything, he was more like the vengeful type.

In any case, she was more than fairly certain that Clancy wouldn't have wanted Ellis Brothers handling the final arrangements for his funeral. He would have rather had her dig a space for him in her parents' backyard and bury him there next to Tania's five hamsters than fall into Tolliver's hands.

Grabbing her coat and purse, Natalya hurried out of her office. An ironic smile twisted her lips. It looked as if she had to come to Clancy's rescue one last time.

* * *

Natalya decided to walk to the Ellis Brothers Mortuary, too impatient to wait for a bus or crowded subway car. It took her a little over a half hour to get there.

Her feet ached. She'd been on them for most of the day, but her indignation pushed all that into the background.

She didn't know what to make of the situation. It was possible, she supposed, that Clancy's mother had had a last-minute change of heart and called the mortuary. If what Clancy had told her about the woman was true, Lucille Donovan had probably whined and begged until Tolliver had finally agreed to do the funeral at a cut rate. And that would be exactly what Clancy would get, cut rate.

Not if she could help it.

The rest of her less than sunny mood could be attributed to good-looking police detectives who kissed and disappeared off the face of the earth.

It irritated her that she hadn't heard one word from DiPalma. Not that she'd expected any undying protestations of affection, but he *had* kissed her, and it had been pretty spectacular on her end. Had it been so awful for him that he'd gone into hiding? There were scores of men she'd seen over the years who would beg to differ with him.

And besides, the detective was supposed to get back to her about her theory that there was something shady going on at Ellis Brothers Mortuary. Had he just been humoring her in order to get her into bed with him, something that had obviously been shelved after he'd kissed and fled.

Natalya raised her collar as she lengthened

her stride and picked up her pace. Her shoulders and elbows were jostled by strangers heading in the opposite direction.

Maybe *fled* was a bit strong, she reconsidered. DiPalma had left at a moderate speed on his motorcycle to go to the scene of a crime. But he might as well have fled since she hadn't heard from him.

It wouldn't be bothering her so much, she argued silently, angling her way through the crowd as she crossed the street, if she wasn't waiting to hear from him about Clancy. After all, Clancy had been murdered.

She needed a clear head to put together the dressing-down she intended to give Tolliver if it turned out that he'd taken it upon himself to claim Clancy's body without Mrs. Donovan's authorization. Even if he was blameless in Clancy's death, he'd still given Clancy a hard time while he was alive and she held that against the man.

By the time she arrived at the two-story gray stone building located in the middle of the block, it had begun to mist. Dewlike drops were clinging to her hair and her coat. It did nothing to improve her mood.

Walking in, Natalya shook off what she could of the rain. A blond receptionist who didn't look as if she had a thought in the world looked up as Natalya entered the somberly lit foyer.

Natalya smoothed down her collar and opened her coat. "I'd like to see Mr. Tolliver, please." A little water from her coat fell on the young woman's desk. The receptionist made a great show of wiping it away.

"I'm sorry, but Mr. Tolliver is presently occupied." She enunciated each word as if she'd memorized it.

Natalya was too keyed up to just stand quietly in the foyer, waiting for Tolliver to finish and be free. She glanced toward the sign on the door behind the young woman. The name plate read Walter Tolliver. She thought she detected the murmur of voices coming through the door.

Good enough for her, Natalya thought.

"This won't take long," she promised, circumventing the woman's desk.

The latter was on her feet instantly, dismay and disbelief both stamped on her smooth face. "But you can't—"

Natalya shot her a cold smile. This was for Clancy. "Oh, but I can," she countered, opening the door. Tolliver, clad in gray, was standing behind his desk. "Mr. Tolliver, you have Clancy Donovan's body—"

She stopped abruptly as she saw the person Tolliver had been talking with turn around.

Mike.

The surprise on his face came and went in less than a heartbeat, to be replaced by tolerant amusement as he nodded toward her. "Dr. Pulaski."

Formal. He was being formal. Was this his way of indicating that they were going to be polite strangers by design, or was this for Tolliver's benefit?

Life, she thought, would definitely be a whole lot simpler if she were a single-cell creature, not given to thought.

Now that she had a moment to get her bearings, Natalya noticed that Tolliver looked decidedly uncomfortable. Because of her? Or because of what Mike was asking him? Either way, she'd stake her life that there was guilt involved.

"Detective DiPalma," she acknowledged.

She kept her voice as pleasant and noncommittal as possible. "Nice to see you again."

"Mr. Tolliver," the receptionist cried. "I'm sorry. I couldn't keep her out."

"No," Natalya said, getting in the man's face. "She couldn't. Would you mind telling me why Clancy is here instead of the mortuary that I selected?"

Tolliver haughtily drew himself up. Straightening his shoulders made him look even thinner than he already did. "I thought, under the circumstances, giving him a decent burial was the only upstanding thing to do. I wasn't aware of any other mortuary being involved."

The man wouldn't know "upstanding" if it ran him over, she thought angrily. And she wasn't buying into his "decent thing to do" act for a second.

"And this is all at your expense." She

couldn't keep the mocking tone out of her voice.

There was suppressed anger in Tolliver's eyes, but he managed to keep it under a lid. Instead, he spread his hands out, the personification of innocence. "Since no one else came forward—"

There was definitely something going on here, she thought. Something more than she could put her finger on right now. But she wasn't about to be fooled, or intimidated, if that was Tolliver's goal.

Her eyes narrowed. She never liked being dismissed or ignored. "I came forward, Mr. Tolliver."

There was frost in his reply. It was obvious that, since she was a friend of Clancy's, he disliked her by association. "I wasn't informed of that."

She half expected Mike to intervene. When he didn't, she assumed he thought she could fight her own battles. She could and she did. "I left word with the coroner's office that I was to be notified once they were satisfied with their autopsy."

There was condescension hanging on every syllable. "There must have been some confusion," Tolliver replied. It was easy to see that he couldn't care less about her part in this, or about the body he'd offered to bury. Which, Mike thought, observing, went along with what the man had told him earlier. He wasn't sure yet if he was buying what Tolliver was selling.

"We do excellent work here," Tolliver assured Natalya.

They cut corners here, according to Clancy. And she believed him before she believed the two-dimensional man standing before her.

"Sorry, I've already made arrangements with another mortuary. They'll be here shortly." She had called the funeral parlor on her way over here, not wanting to waste any time. The receptionist assured her that the car would be there to pick up "the deceased" within the hour.

It was still hard for her to think of Clancy that way. And having to deal with this reptile in an expensive suit didn't help any.

A small sigh of exasperation escaped Tolliver's lips. He inclined his head. "As you wish." Then, as if Natalya didn't even exist, he turned his eyes toward Mike. "Are we done here, Detective?"

He'd gotten a few answers he wanted to explore. "Yes. For now," Mike qualified. The fact that Tolliver shifted ever so slightly and looked uncomfortable with the addition of the second sentence was not lost on him.

Mike looked at Natalya. There was fire in her eyes. No matter what he tried to tell himself to the contrary, the woman was magnificent. He'd wanted to call her the morning following the Central Park homicide that had taken him away from her. But the very fact that he wanted to call her as much as he did had kept him from doing it. The intensity of his desire unnerved him and put him on his guard. He thought some space might put things in perspective.

But, looking at her now, he realized that he'd been wrong. Space did nothing but increase the longing. Out of sight, out of mind definitely did not apply here.

"I'll walk you out," he offered, joining her. "Unless you have something else you want to say to Mr. Tolliver."

There was a lot she wanted to say to Tolliver, but she doubted that any of it would make an impression. Better not to waste words. The only thing the man understood was money. The best she could do was find out who had originally authorized that Ellis Brothers take care of burial arrangements for the city's nameless dead and see what could be done about transferring that business somewhere else.

"No," she replied, turning on her heel.

"Wait, you're walking too fast," Mike called after her as he lengthened his stride. "In a hurry to get somewhere?" he wanted to know.

She didn't bother turning around, not wanting to see Tolliver again. "Just out of here, for one."

"And for two?" Mike asked when she didn't follow up her statement.

Natalya pressed her lips together. She didn't answer. Even though she wanted to know why he hadn't called, she couldn't ask. Instead, she focused on why he'd come to see Tolliver in the first place.

They walked down the short corridor to the

front door. The mist outside appeared to be gone, after having left its mark on the glass doors.

"I was beginning to think that you weren't going to question Tolliver."

He'd spent the last half hour questioning the man, tendering questions as subtly as he could so as not to alarm the director. He didn't know if he linked Tolliver with the murder, but he knew he didn't like him, period. Mike made a mental note to check out the man's alibi. The funeral director had said that he'd spent the evening sitting with the Wallace family, predominantly comforting Wallace's bereaved widow.

"You had an interesting theory," Mike reminded her.

Natalya could feel the excitement taking hold, pouring through her veins. "And?"

But Mike was already shaking his head. "So far, Tolliver's books are above reproach. He's filed his taxes on time and we've checked out all the grave sites that were mentioned." An utterly ghoulish thing to do, he thought. "There are graves for every single body Ellis Brothers charged the city for."

There had to be something. She couldn't shake the feeling that Tolliver was behind all this. "How deep did you dig?"

"Deep." He saw disappointment warring with eternal optimism in her eyes. He supposed she needed that to be a successful doctor, a way to battle the hopelessness. He smiled at her. "Don't worry, if Tolliver is re-sponsible, we'll get him."

Was he just patronizing her? "How?"

That was the million-dollar question. One for which he had no answer. But he would. "The law moves in mysterious ways, Doc."

"That's the Lord," she corrected. "The *Lord*

moves in mysterious ways." For a second, he'd actually had her going.

About to say something, she stopped. The look in his eyes was impossible to fathom. All she knew was that he wasn't putting her on. Or putting her off, either. Maybe there was reason to hope.

Running into her like this had his hormones revving up. If he didn't know better, he would have said he was fifteen. What he did know was that he didn't want to just walk away from her now that fate had thrown them together again.

"Can I give you a lift somewhere? I still owe you dinner."

Could he do that, just pick up and do what he wanted? "Aren't you on duty?"

He shook his head. "I've been off duty for the last hour."

She was confused. Natalya looked over her

shoulder at the awning of the building they had just left. "But you were in there, question-ing Tolliver." She stopped, the answer dawning on her. "You were questioning him on your own time?"

The other case was taking priority, but he felt he owed it to her. Bottom line was that he hated letting anyone get away with murder. "City's cutting back on overtime and there is only so much I can do during regular hours."

"That homicide you were called away takes precedence?" she guessed.

He wanted her to understand that it just wasn't a whim. "Third homeless person slaughtered in two months. The captain put a priority on it."

Homeless people. Obviously no rich, fat-cat relatives with political clout were putting the screws to the department to solve the crimes. It heartened her to know that about the city she lived in. Despite what this meant to Clancy's unsolved murder, she smiled, nodding. "Sounds like a nice man, your captain."

Mike laughed to himself. "You'd be the first to think so. Captain Sorenson's a tough son of a bitch. I don't think he ever goes home except to change clothes. Otherwise, he lives in the office."

They were walking around to the back of the building, where the mortuary had its small parking lot. More parking was provided two blocks down but Mike's motorcycle required a minimum of space.

"I take it he's not married," Natalya guessed.

"Not anymore. Marriage and the department is a tough combination."

"Don't say that." The request was only half-teasing. "My sister's marrying one of your own next month."

"There're exceptions," Mike allowed. He

knew, if he ever finally settled down, nothing that crossed his path would be allowed to come home with him. The kinds of things he saw on the job had no place in his private life. He stopped by his motorcycle. "So, how about it? Are you up for dinner?"

She wanted to. God, but she wanted to. Wanted to spend some time with this good-looking detective that God and, indirectly, Clancy, kept throwing her way. But not tonight. Not unless she was completely irresponsible. And those days were behind her.

With deep regret, Natalya looked at her watch, hoping against hope that time had somehow magically stood still and was affording her an island upon which to indulge herself.

No such luck. She was already running late. Sasha was going to have her head on a platter—not to mention what Mama would say.

She looked up at him ruefully. "Only if it comes in a bag to go."

He was trying to read between the lines. "You're in the mood for a picnic?"

She laughed. "Not in November. I'm late for my fitting. It's the maid-of-honor dress," she explained. "My sister Sasha's wedding."

The ob-gyn, he remembered. "Right, to the police detective."

"Right." The impulse came out of nowhere, roaring down the middle of her life. Why not? "Would you like to come?"

She certainly wasn't the easiest woman to follow, he decided. "To the fitting?"

He'd be bored out of his mind. And Mama would pounce on him. "No, to the wedding."

Was she asking him as her date? Or just throwing the doors open to a big family cele-bration as her way of thanking him for his interest in her friend? He knew it was the kind of thing his family would do, but Italians didn't have a lock on rampaging hospitality.

He considered refusing for a second. After all, he wouldn't know anyone but her and he normally steered clear of weddings unless he was roped into standing up for the groom.

But there was something about her eyes…

Hell, why not? "Sure. When is it?" She gave him the date, which was a little over three weeks away. He never scheduled things that far in advance. "Barring another homicide, I'm free."

"Good, I'll call and give you details later."

"Details?" Was this going to get compli-cated? He wasn't sure if he wanted it to or not. Wasn't sure of anything, really, except that he could have stood and basked in her pleased ex-pression all night.

"Where, when, things like that." She looked

at him intently, raising the collar of her coat again. The cold was beginning to get to her. "But right now, I'm going to have to get going."

"Where is this maid-of-honor dress place?"

His phrasing had her smile widening. She liked him. Liked him a lot. Natalya rattled off an address in Queens. The woman who ran the shop had come over on the boat with her parents and they had struck up a friendship, giving each other support during the very lean years. Periodically Mama had tried to match each one of them up with the woman's less than cheerful son, Peter. Mercifully, Papa had finally made her see that Peter would *not* have been a good addition to the family.

Mike straddled his bike, then held out a helmet for her. "Hop on."

She took the helmet and slipped it on, fastening the strap. Her skirt had to be hiked up somewhat before she could get on the bike behind him. She caught him watching appreciatively.

"Fringe benefit," he told her before he turned to face forward.

She slipped her arms around his waist. It occurred to her that she liked the sensation that passed through her. "Let's go."

The words were barely out of her mouth before they were flying down the street.

Chapter 9

"And who was that?"

Natalya nearly jumped out of her skin. She hadn't realized that her mother was anywhere in the vicinity when Mike dropped her off at the bridal shop entrance. Looking back, she should have known better. Her mother *always* managed to materialize out of thin air. When they were little girls, she and Sasha had been convinced that Magda Pulaski had magical powers.

Turning around, she realized too late that she was still smiling as she looked at the petite woman standing with the door half-ajar. "That was the police detective investigating Clancy's murder."

Magda Pulaski came forward and squinted as she focused intently on the figure that was becoming little more than a dark silhouette as he disappeared down the street.

"Do all investigating police detectives giving rides to the friends of the dead person?" she asked her daughter innocently.

"'Give,' Mama, do all investigating police detectives 'give' rides to the friends of—" With a sigh, Natalya gave up trying to fix the sentence. "The answer is no, Mama. They don't."

A knowing expression feathered across her face. "Ah."

Natalya held the door open for her mother as she entered the building. "No 'ah'."

Magda spread her hands, looking mystified at the rejoinder. "What no 'ah?' 'Ah' is 'ah,'" she said simply. "Nothing more."

If only that were true, Natalya thought. "That's right, Mama, *nothing more*," she emphasized.

Magda's expression was just this side of smug. "He is not looking like nothing more. He is looking like 'something' more. His eyes—"

Okay, now she had her. Her mother was making this up as she went along. "You couldn't possibly see his eyes from where you were standing, Mama."

Magda took offense. "I could seeing everything from where I was standing. My eyes, they are seeing like when I was a young girl."

Natalya sighed. She scanned the small, crowded store for her sisters, hoping one of them would come to her rescue. They had to be in the back, she decided. It figured. "Go, turn those sharp eyes on Papa, Mama," Natalya half pleaded.

Magda gave a delicate but dismissive snort. "Your father, he is home, hiding. All things female make him nervous."

She had a feeling that it was her mother that made her father nervous. Her mother was un-predictable. At a time in life where most people settled into a pattern, her mother was like a firecracker, set to go off. "Then he certainly got into the wrong family, didn't he, Mama?"

"Yes, poor man." Magda chuckled. Slipping her arm around her daughter's waist, she beamed at her second born. She was enjoying herself immensely. One of her girls was getting married. Only four more to go. "Come, your sisters, they are in the back.

Should we telling them about your investigating detective?"

Natalya prayed for patience and wished she'd taken the subway instead of letting Mike bring her. "There's nothing to tell."

An expression most recently seen on a cat after swallowing a mouse visited her mother's face. "Of course there is not."

Her mother was the only woman she knew who let you know she was disagreeing with you while she was agreeing.

Natalya gave up.

"God bless technology and nosy citizens," Louis cried with feeling, the words erupting from his mouth like a victorious war cry.

Mike looked up from the pile of notes that he'd been drowning in, his interest immediately piqued. At this point, diversion for any reason was more than welcomed. He and Louis had been fielding phone calls from people all morning. The calls poured in immediately following the captain's appearance on the six o'clock news. After a brief prepared statement, Sorenson had asked for the public's help in regards to the mysterious deaths of homeless men.

Who said New Yorkers were disinterested and cold? Mike thought. It seemed as if half the population had called in, saying they "thought" they might have seen something out of the ordinary. That, he mused, pretty much described life in the city on a day-to-day basis.

About to pick up the receiver to take yet another call, Mike replaced it in its cradle and rubbed the shell of his ear. Right now, it felt as if he'd had both ears glued to the receiver for an entire decade instead of the last four hours.

"What?" he demanded, hoping it was something they could work with and not just Louis making a random comment about the country's state of affairs.

If the smile on Louis's face were any wider, it would have cracked his lips. "Seems a passerby got a home movie of the last murder."

It sounded as if they were finally catching a break, but Mike knew not to get too excited until he heard everything. Louis tended to get carried away. He was the optimist in their partnership. As for Mike, he'd always been a realist. In addition, the job had taught him that nothing was ever what it seemed.

"So how much does he or she want for this home movie?"

If he detected Mike's skepticism, Louis gave no indication. This was the first real break that they'd caught in relation to the three senseless murders. "That's just it. It's a tourist—some guy here for the first time with his wife—and they want to, quote—" he paused dramatically "—'do the right thing.'"

Mike frowned. "What's that mean? They're willing to charge us the going rate for film instead of selling the video to the highest bidder?"

Louis shook his head so hard, the ends of his unruly hair swung back and forth. "No, he and his wife are *giving* it to us."

Mike stared at his partner in disbelief. Even so, he was on his feet, slipping on his leather jacket. "You're kidding."

Louis got up, taking his jacket off the back of his chair, never breaking eye contact. Mike found himself thinking that if his partner were any happier, he would have been levitating an inch off the ground.

"Never on an empty stomach." He tugged his jacket on, falling into step beside Mike. "Which reminds me, I haven't had lunch yet."

"It's eleven o'clock," Mike pointed out, nodding at the clock on the wall as they passed it.

"Exactly." Louis went out the door first, then turned to look at him. "You buying?"

Mike laughed shortly. He wasn't ready to start celebrating just yet. Louis was older by half a decade, but Mike was the more jaded of the two. He'd stopped believing in Santa Claus at five, much to his mother's dismay. "If this film turns out to be the real thing, I'll buy you a steak, Louis."

"Don't toy with me like that, DiPalma." Louis's voice echoed down the stairwell. "You know how that kind of talk gets my gastric juices flowing."

Mike shook his head. "You're a walking stomach, Louis. Your gastric juices are *always* flowing. Let's go get us a video."

The video turned out to be genuine, as was the couple. Visiting New York to celebrate their twenty-fifth anniversary, Mae and Raymond Applegate, from Grand Forks, North Dakota, were only too happy to help in the investigation.

"Will there be a commendation? Ray deserves a commendation," his wife, a slightly heavyset woman, said with zeal. Her husband tried to hush her.

"I'll take it up with the captain," Mike promised. "Just give my partner your address. And we'll be returning the tape when we're finished with it."

"Keep it as long as you need," Raymond urged. "I'm just happy to help."

Didn't meet people like that every day, Mike thought as they left the hotel room.

Didn't meet women like Natalya, either.

The thought had just popped up and he buried it the moment it did. He had a tape to authenticate. There was no time to think about a woman who took his breath away.

Later at the precinct, the computer wizard that the department retained verified that the video surrendered by the Applegates hadn't been doctored in any way.

"Can you see anything?" was Mike's next question to the technician, since the videos most amateur filmmakers made tended to be shots of their feet and out-of-range tourist attractions.

"Well, it was pretty grainy," Leonard said, pushing his hair out of his eyes. "So it took a little doing to enhance it."

"Enhance it?" Louis echoed.

"In this case, make it clearer. It was shot in the evening, with pretty poor lighting. The streetlamp in the area appeared to be out, so at first, all you see is shadows."

"And at second?" Mike wanted to know.

"Well, you be the judge," Leonard urged. Louis and Mike flanked him on either side as he struck several keys on the keyboard. The tape began to play on the wide-screen monitor.

There were three men in the grainy footage, two assailants and their victim. Only one of the assailants could be marginally identified. Atypical of other cases around the country, the two men who were attacking the homeless man didn't seem to be doing it for the thrill of the kill. Nor were they doing it to rob a person who owned nothing but the shoes on his feet.

"Hey, freeze that," Louis ordered. He leaned

in closer, examining what was on the monitor. One of the men was kneeling over the homeless victim. "Is he stabbing that guy in slow motion?"

Leonard adjusted his rimless glasses, moving the video frame by frame. "Sure looks that way." A few more strokes of the keys brought the picture even more into focus. Not satisfied, Leonard enlarged it to the next level.

Mike stood behind Louis, his arms crossed as he studied the footage intently. "Wait, freeze it again." Leonard did as he asked. "That's not a stab." Excitement finally began to bubble in his veins. Mike pointed at the screen. "That's an incision."

"An incision?" Louis squinted despite being a foot away from the monitor. Confusion creased his rounded face and he looked at Mike over Leonard's head. "He practicing to be a doctor?"

Leonard had resumed playing the video. Mike watched intently. There were only a few seconds left. "Whatever he was doing, they were scared away by our tourist with the camera." He nodded at the tech. "Thanks, Leo. Print up a couple of copies."

"Will do," Leonard agreed, as Mike began to walk out of the darkened room.

"Where are you going?" Louis wanted to know as he hurried after him, lengthening his strides in order to catch up.

Watching the video had made him think of something. It was a long shot, but this was a job based on long shots. "Back to the M.E."

Donald Ruiz, the medical examiner, was far from happy to see the two detectives return since he knew it meant reopening a case. He greeted their appearance with a sigh that seemed to come from the bottom of his size twelve feet.

"To what do I owe this visit?" the older man asked sarcastically.

Mike got right to it. "We need you to dig up the reports on those three homeless victims that were killed in the last four months."

"I sent out copies," Ruiz said stubbornly. But the staring contest between Mike and the M.E. was short-lived. The man threw up his hands. "And you'd be looking for what?"

Mike believed in having a decent working relationship with everyone, but he and the M.E. had never hit it off. "Something missing."

"You mean like personal items?" It was obvious that the M.E. was thinking the police helped themselves to whatever might have been found on the men's bodies before they were brought to his table.

"More like bodily effects," Louis corrected.

"Or body parts," Mike added.

The M.E.'s jaw slackened slightly as he abandoned his initial resistance. "Now that you mention it, the first guy came in with only one kidney and the second didn't have his spleen."

"And you didn't think this was anything unusual?" Mike asked, incredulously.

Ruiz immediately became defensive. "You can lose a spleen in an auto accident. I figured the other guy maybe sold his kidney to get some money to buy his booze. Black market, that sort of thing."

"And the third victim?" Mike pressed.

The medial examiner smirked, vindicated. "Everything was there. Liver was shot, but everything else looked to be in working order." Shaggy eyebrows drew together in a scowl.

"It's all there in the report I dictated," he grounded out.

Mike wasn't ready to give up just yet. "How about an incision?"

Ruiz looked at the two men as if they'd just suggested going on a weekend trip to the Arctic. "What?"

"A fresh incision," Mike specified. "Some tourist gave up a video he took. He caught the last murder on tape."

Ruiz looked duly impressed. Eighty percent of the department's cases were solved because of luck but coming up against it was always a bit numbing. "Damn."

"Yeah, our sentiments exactly," Mike agreed. "It looked as if one of the murderers was making an incision when our amateur Steven Spielberg caught him in the act and he and his partner fled."

Curiosity got the best of him. The M.E. temporarily abandoned his belligerent attitude. "What are you thinking?"

Mike threw out one viable theory. "Could be cannibalism."

Louis's eyes widened so far it looked as if they were in danger of falling out of his head. "You mean like in *Silence of the Lambs*?"

He was thinking more along the lines of a Jeffery Dahmer kind of spree, which chilled his heart a great deal more than any movie plot conceived in Hollywood. But he knew that Louis liked to separate himself from his work through the magic of movies.

"Yeah." He advanced a second, possibly more likely theory. "Or body parts for sale. There's good money in that."

"I vote for the second," Louis said, just barely stifling the shiver that coursed down his broad, square back.

Mike nodded. He was leaning toward that himself. "Either way, there're going to be more homeless people in jeopardy with more to worry about than just the coming winter."

Ruiz shook his head. "That's why I like working with the dead," he confided. "The living are too complicated. Wait here. I'll get the reports," he promised. He was back in less than five minutes. "I made copies," he volunteered, indicating the pages he handed over.

Mike nodded as he took them. "Thanks."

As they left the building, he glanced at his watch. "Damn."

"Battery die?" Louis wanted to know.

"No." Abruptly, he handed the reports over to Louis. "Take these back to the squad room." Stepping into the street, he held his hand up for the benefit of the cab in the distance. "I'm late."

Louis stared at him, bewildered. "For?"

"I'm taking some personal time," Mike told him. The cab pulled up practically at his feet. Mike opened the door. "Already cleared it with the captain."

"I'm your partner," Louis complained as Mike got into the taxi. It was a known fact that Louis hated being left out of anything. "You're supposed to share."

"I'll bring back doughnuts. We'll share that," Mike promised, his words trailing after him through the open window. He gave the driver the address as the man pulled away from the curb.

Because of traffic, Mike missed the service. But he managed to make it to the cemetery before the priest arrived.

Paying off the driver, he got out of the cab and began to walk across the field. He could see a number of people gathered around the open grave site. stopped beside a headstone with an angel arched on it.

He'd wanted to be there for Natalya, but it looked like a lot of people had had the same thought. She didn't really need him, he told himself. If he were smart, he'd just double back across the field and leave.

Looking at the faces of the five women around her, he figured they had to be Natalya's family. Although there appeared to be six different shades of hair colors, the features were close enough to label them as sisters. All except for the shortest one. She had deep black, straight hair, worn short in a style that seemed to pop up every decade or so. It vaguely reminded him of a Dutch boy. The more rounded figure and somewhat older face told him that she was probably Natalya's mother. Although the woman didn't look all that much older than her daughters.

Mike was about to retreat from the cemetery when Natalya suddenly looked up. Their eyes met and held. He watched surprise, and then pleasure, wash over her face. Even at this distance, it managed to send chills down his spine.

Was she like that when she made love? Or was she so skilled at the art that nothing surprised her?

Whoa! Where did that come from?

He was standing in a cemetery, for God's sake. You weren't supposed to have those kinds of thoughts in a cemetery.

He saw her say something to the woman beside her and suddenly they were all looking at him. All six women and the one lone man who stood among them.

Natalya's father, he guessed.

The escape he'd meant to make slipped through his fingers. Detected, he had no recourse but to stay where he was as Natalya made her way to him.

She laced her arm through his the moment she joined him. "I didn't expect you to come."

"I thought maybe you needed someone." He looked at the group she'd just left. "Not exactly an original thought I guess."

"That's just my family," she told him needlessly. "They all knew Clancy. And liked him. He didn't have to put on his act around them," she added. "I knew he'd like seeing them come to his funeral."

Mike looked at her for a long moment. What was it like to have that kind of faith? Much to his mother's dismay, that sort of belief didn't enter into his life. "You believe that."

"With all my heart," she said with feeling, then looked up at him, curious. "Why? Don't you?"

"My mother says, if I'm not careful, I'll wind up in hell." His mouth curved slightly. "I'd be worried if I believed there was such a place."

"I don't know about hell, but I know there's a heaven."

Natalya sounded absolutely certain. He couldn't help the amusement that came into his eyes. "You've got proof."

"Yes." Natalya tapped her heart. "In here. I've felt it. But you didn't come here to talk theology—or lack thereof."

"No," he admitted. "I came for you." He realized from her smile that he had said that out loud.

Belatedly he noticed that not only was she holding on to his arm, but she was leading him back to where her family was standing. The priest had arrived and he had taken his place at the head of the grave, his Bible opened to his selection.

The protest that might have come never surfaced. After all, he'd come to the funeral to give her moral support. He might as well take his place by her side—despite the fact that he was being scrutinized by seven sets of eyes. Even the priest sent a penetrating look his way before beginning to read.

In a soft cadence, the priest said the words that would accompany Natalya's childhood friend to his final resting place. For her sake, Mike did his best to look as if he believed in what was being said.

Chapter 10

The service was brief, simple. Just the way she knew that Clancy would have wanted it.

All the while, Natalya was very aware of the tall man standing beside her.

After the service, she quickly introduced Mike to her mother and sisters. Out of the corner of her eye, she saw her father slip the priest an envelope, a gratuity for his time. She silently blessed him. Her father was one in a million. Both her parents were.

But that didn't mean she was going to allow her mother to have her chance at Mike.

Very subtly, she slipped her arm through his and began walking toward the parking lot. "Thank you for coming," she whispered. "You didn't have to, but it was really very nice of you."

He didn't want her making a big deal out of it. For one thing, he'd wanted to see her again, however briefly. He just hadn't realized that her whole family would be there.

Mike shrugged, passing off her words. "Seemed like the right thing to do."

"I'm having everyone over to the apartment for some sandwiches and coffee." She stopped walking and looked up at him. His presence made the overcast day feel a little less dreary. "Nothing fancy. You're welcome to come."

He would have been tempted—if the word *everyone* wasn't part of the invitation. And besides, he'd only signed out for a couple of hours. "Thanks, but I have to be getting back."

"Of course." She'd forgotten about that. The funeral had thrown everything off-kilter for her. She had another doctor covering for her today. She knew her sisters had done the same.

Natalya resumed walking, tucking her arm back through his. When they reached the parking lot, she was aware that her family was behind her, but their pace had been slower so they hadn't caught up yet.

"Did you find out anything when you talked to Tolliver? I know you're not supposed to talk about an ongoing investigation, but…" She let her voice trail off. And then she lifted her head, raising her eyes to his.

The hope he saw there was hard to miss. He

found himself getting imprisoned in the green orbs without hope of parole.

She wasn't going to like this, he thought. He hadn't mentioned it to her because he knew it would make her angry. But maybe she deserved to know. "Tolliver told me that he was getting ready to fire Clancy."

This was a surprise. There'd been no love lost between the two, but Clancy had been a good worker, had taken pride in doing the best job possible no matter what it was. "Fire him? Why?"

"Tolliver said it was because of improper behavior on Clancy's part."

Clancy had known better than to hit on anyone he worked with. Not everyone was as tolerant of his ways as she was.

"With who?" she wanted to know.

He hadn't realized how hard it would be to

tell her, to shatter whatever image she had of her friend. But he couldn't not tell her at this point. "Some of the bodies he prepared for embalming."

Her eyes widened in horror. Outrage was swift and immediate. The bastard, spreading stories about Clancy now, when he couldn't stand up for himself.

"Necrophilia? Clancy wasn't like that." Indignation vibrated in her voice. "He liked partners who were breathing. What a disgusting thing for Tolliver to say. He's throwing up a smoke screen," she insisted. "To hide whatever it is that he's up to."

Mike had his doubts about that. "Natalya, are you sure that Clancy maybe—"

Her eyes narrowed, drawing her eyebrows together. "Don't even finish it," she warned. "Tolliver's lying. I would stake my life on it.

And if he's lying about this, then he's probably lying about other things." It only made sense to her. "Clancy said he was on to something—" she reminded him.

Mike nodded. "Yes, I know." And he had pulled every string on that he could. "But there wasn't anything underhanded about the books. Every charge, every body was accounted for."

She refused to give up. "Then it's something else." She tried to think, desperate to pull a rabbit out of a hat. And then it suddenly hit her. "Maybe Tolliver's selling body parts. Maybe—"

Mike looked at her sharply, his head snapping up. "What did you say?"

"Maybe he's selling body parts," she repeated. Having caught his interest, her mind raced to find embellishments. "Like the urban legends. You know, people getting killed so that body parts could be harvested. Body parts for dying, rich people who would be willing to pay any price for a kidney or a new heart or a lung—" She realized she was getting carried away. She didn't want him to think that he was talking to a lunatic. "Sorry, I didn't mean to babble."

"I wouldn't exactly call it babbling." His expression was thoughtful. "Besides, maybe you are on to something."

"I am?" She could see he wasn't just humoring her. "What do you know?" she asked eagerly.

But he had already said too much. He straddled his motorcycle. "I've really got to go." And he did. He needed some time to think. There were pieces he needed to find and match up.

He was about to start his motorcycle, but he had hesitated a bit too long. Apparently thinking she'd stood on the sidelines too long, Natalya's mother finally made her way over to them.

She smiled broadly at Mike. It was one of the kindest smiles he had ever seen. "Natalya, maybe your young man, he would like to be coming with us? Have something to eat?" The woman looked at him with hazel eyes that seemed to draw him in.

He saw where Natalya got it from. The woman must have been something else when she was younger. The beauty, a little faded, was still there, like a lingering melody of an old popular song that could still stir feelings when played.

"That's a tempting offer, Mrs. Pulaski," he told her, "but I have to get back to work."

Magda was not deterred. "Perhaps I could call your boss—"

Natalya cut in, knowing that the longer Mike hesitated, the tighter her mother's web was spun. "She would, too." She tapped the motorcycle handle. "Quick, make your getaway before it's too late."

"Natalya." Magda pursed her lips. "Is this a way to talking about your mother?"

Natalya spread her hands wide. "If the shoe fits…"

Her mother looked down at her footwear, confusion gracing her brows. "My shoes fit."

Natalya laughed for the first time that day. "Never mind, Mama." Nodding at Mike, she slipped her arm around her mother's shoulders. "Thanks for coming."

"Right." With a pending sense of urgency, he started up his motorcycle. He saw Natalya's mother eyeing his bike with interest and approval as the rest of the family came to join her. Time to go, he thought.

"We have a wedding," Magda called after him, raising her voice. "Would you like to come?"

He turned just before leaving the lot. "Already said yes."

Magda clapped her hands together. "Wonderful." She looked at Natalya meaningfully.

Natalya rolled her eyes. "I'd like to go home and die now, Mama."

Her mother shook her head, frowning. "Such a thing to saying. When you have everything to live for." They began to walk to their own vehicle. "What did you say his name was?"

Her father, bless him, came to her rescue. Or tried to. "Magda, leave the girl alone."

Magda shrugged away her husband's request. "If she had wanted to be left alone, she should have been born an orphan."

The funny thing was, Natalya thought as she opened the rear passenger door of her father's car, her mother actually believed that.

* * *

Sasha looked at her reflection in the mirror. Daylight came through a small, stained-glass window, pushing its way into the room. She pressed her hand against the delicate lace that lay against her empty, knotted stomach.

Makeup or not, she looked pale, she thought. Pale enough to pass for Snow White. Snow White about to have a nervous breakdown.

The vestibule within St. Joseph's Church was crowded with her sisters, wearing pale blue, floor-length bridesmaid dresses, and her mother, who was stunning in a sapphire blue gown. It seemed to Sasha as if they were all talking at once, their voices dissolving into a sea of chatter. She couldn't make out a single word.

Her head was spinning.

Magda came up behind her, giving her arm a squeeze. Their eyes met in the mirror. There was concern on her mother's face.

That made two of them, Sasha thought. Was this a mistake? Would all her happiness dissolve the moment she said "I do"? She loved Tony, but she just didn't know if this was the right thing. She didn't want to love just to lose. Not again.

Sasha blew out a breath, still pressing against her abdomen. "I don't think I was this nervous even before I delivered my first baby."

"Everyone is afraid," Magda assured her. Her voice was kind, yet authoritative. "It is only normal." She winked. "Remember, my darling, the first one hundred years are the hardest. After that—" she waved one hand grandly "—piece of bread."

"Cake, Mama, I think you mean cake,"

Natalya interjected as she threaded her way through her sisters to Sasha's other side.

Magda's small shoulders rose and fell carelessly. "Cake, bread, what is the difference? You can eating both." And then she looked at Sasha, her heart swelling. She took her face between her hands. "You were his before he ever asked you to be."

Sasha looked at her mother for a very long moment. And then she smiled. "You just want to have grandchildren."

Magda inclined her head. "There is that, too."

"Well, the priest is going to have a cow if we're not all out there in a couple of minutes," Natalya informed them after glancing at her watch. "He has another wedding in an hour."

"Drive-through weddings have finally hit New York," Tania quipped with a laugh.

"Let's go, let's go," Natalya urged, shooing

her mother and sisters out of the room. "Take your positions." Only when the vestibule had cleared did she turn to Sasha to snare one last moment alone with her sister before she became Tony's wife. "God, but you are beautiful. I'd hug you but I'd wind up crushing the lace on your bodice."

Right now, human contact would be more than welcomed. "What's a little crushed lace between sisters?" She put out her arms. "I need a hug."

Natalya obliged, then stood back and looked at her older sister in wonder. "Sasha, you're shaking."

Sasha took another deep breath then let it out, trying to steady her pulse. "Maybe I need a shot of whiskey besides the hug."

Natalya shook her head as she began to fuss with Sasha's veil. "What you need, O lion, is to tap into your courage. You love him, he loves you. God and Mama—not necessarily in that order—just want to make it official, that's all." She stopped and looked at her sister. "Tony's a good guy, Sash. He'll make you happy." And then she grinned. "And if he doesn't, threaten him with Mama. That'll put the fear of God into him." Natalya suddenly paused, cocking her head as she listened. "They're playing your song, kid." She nodded toward the doorway. "Time to make an honest man out of Tony."

But as they started to leave the room, Sasha stopped her for a second, placing her hand on her arm. "I love you, Nat."

"Yeah, I know." And then she looked down at the hand that was still on her arm. "I also know that if you don't get yourself moving, you're going to die of frostbite. God, your hands are cold. Let's go and have Tony warm you up."

Natalya hustled her sister out of the vestibule carefully holding up her train and veil. She wanted nothing getting in the way of her sister's wedding.

The music, warm and sensual, wrapped itself around them. It was a song Mike vaguely recognized, although the words were missing. What mattered was that the song was slow and that he was holding Natalya in his arms.

He could feel her breathing. His gut tightened as her breasts softly rose and fell against his chest with each breath she took. It was hard to keep from squeezing her hand as he held it tucked against him.

"What?" Natalya asked. When he raised a silent eyebrow, questioning her query, she said, "You have a funny expression on your face."

Had to be all the feelings scrambling inside of him. But he wasn't about to admit anything just yet. This was too new and as far as he knew, it could fade away the next moment.

So he went with flattery, because that had always seen him in good stead. "I didn't realize just how pretty you were until just now." Which was the truth. Seeing her in the formfitting blue gown, flowers in her hair, had hit him with both barrels. "I'd say that you are the prettiest one here."

Her eyes held mischief in them, there was no other way to describe it. "You mean other than you?"

Her response was unexpected. She'd thrown him for a loop. "What?"

"Mama thinks you're pretty," she told him. She knew that wherever Magda was in the large ballroom, her mother was watching her. "Maybe a little too pretty."

He wasn't sure how to take the comment. Maybe where Natalya's mother came from, that was a compliment. "Never had anyone's mother say that before."

Natalya's smile began in her eyes. There was deep affection in her voice. "Mama's kind of in a class by herself. Not to mention outspoken."

Mike laughed as he nodded in agreement. "Yeah, I noticed." He realized that Natalya made no protest as he tightened his hold around her waist, drawing her closer. "You know, I wasn't really sure just what to expect, coming here."

She knew all about the stereotypical image he was undoubtedly laboring under.

"This can't be your first wedding, so I'm guessing this is your first Polish wedding." Amusement filtered all through her. She'd long since stopped taking offense. Humor was a great defuser. "Were you looking for accordions?"

Actually, he had, but he knew to say so might be insulting to her since it was so utterly stereotypical. Still, he didn't want to actually lie, either. So he shrugged casually as the music continued to weave seductively around them. "Maybe not accordions, but at least a few polkas."

"Wait, they'll come." Her father had insisted on it, saying it couldn't be a real Polish wedding without at least one decent polka. He intended to dance it with Sasha. "And a tarantella, as well." She saw a smattering of disbelief cross Mike's face. "Tony's Italian, remember?" Her parents deeply believed in honoring heritage as well as their adopted country. "New York City is just a huge melting pot, after all."

He caught himself hoping that the music—this song—would go on forever. So he could remain like this, with an excuse to continue holding her in his arms.

"Or so they taught us in fourth grade history," he recalled. But she deserved his honest thoughts on the subject. "In my experience, people of different nationalities like to preserve their heritage, not mingle with other cultures." He looked down at her face. "You can't tell me that your mother wouldn't rather have your sister marry some nice, upstanding Polish guy."

He didn't get it, did he? That wasn't what either of her parents were about. Heritage took a backseat to their children's best interests and happiness. "My mother wants Sasha to be happy. If Sasha would have been happy marrying a Chia Pet, Mama would have given her blessings. After the pysch exam, of course," Natalya added after a beat.

Mike laughed out loud, attracting the attention of several of the couples around them on the floor. "Chia Pet, huh? I guess maybe I underestimated your mother."

"I guess maybe you did," she agreed. Her eyes dancing, she told him, "People only do that once."

He could see that. Still, it sounded rather ominous. "You make her sound like a CIA operative."

Instead of laughing it off, Natalya looked serious for a moment. "A lot of blank spaces as far as my parents are concerned. For the most part, they're very open people, but I have a feeling that they both went through a great deal that they're not talking about. When they 'left' Poland, their government wasn't into issuing travel visas."

"Maybe you shouldn't be telling me this." For the Pulaskis' sake, he didn't want to know more. He didn't want to be put in a position to choose between his badge and his conscience.

She looked up at him, confused. "Why?"

Did she need it spelled out for her? He searched her face and saw no guile there. Apparently, she *did* need it spelled out.

"Natalya, if your parents are here illegally—"

She stopped him before he could continue. "Oh, they're here legally. I can show you their citizenship papers." They were framed and hung over the piano that her father sometimes played. "How they left their homeland, however, might not have received the stamp of approval from their government at the time. Now, with the democracy in place, it's another story."

He felt oddly relieved and dismissed the

feeling, telling himself it was just that he didn't like complications, nothing more.

"Have either of them gone back?" His grand-mother used to dream of returning to her place of birth. Toward the end, just before she died, she had talked of it constantly.

Natalya shook her head. "Neither one wants to. This is their home now."

When the song ended he reluctantly let his hand slip from her waist. "No relatives for them to visit back there?"

"Not that they talk about."

Any further questions he was thinking of asking were curtailed as a shushing sound moved through the ballroom like a wave, washing over everyone and pushing them into silence. Sasha's father walked up before the band and took one of the microphones in his hand. A high-pitched, piercing noise zipped

through the room, causing many to involun-
tarily wince.

Josef looked sheepish. "Oh, sorry. My
wedding ring." Switching hands, he held up
the offending one for everyone to see before
dropping it to his side again. "It is time for the
bride to be throwing her very expensive
flowers to someone. All the not-married
women, please to coming closer," he urged,
gesturing to the crowd.

As a sea of women converged before
Natalya's father, Mike noticed that Natalya
remained where she was. He leaned his head
in toward her.

"Something you want to tell me?" he asked.
When she raised one inquisitive eyebrow, he
elaborated. "You're not joining the group of
'not-married women.'"

She hadn't planned on it, but now, with him

looking at her, something made her want to join in. So she shrugged. "I guess I'd better."

"Okay, Sasha, no favorites," Josef instructed. He used his hands to accompany his words, gesturing for her to turn away. "Turn and looking at the wall, please."

"Yes, Daddy," Sasha said dutifully, laughing. Turning to face the band, she pitched her bouquet up high, aiming it as best she could behind her.

The women who had gathered together for this event surged forward as if they were one. Only Natalya remained standing where she was.

She merely raised her hands in self-defense when she saw the flowers coming straight at her.

Chapter 11

Sometimes, Natalya thought, it seemed to her that things just happened without any preplanning.

For instance, she'd had no intention of catching Sasha's wedding bouquet, yet there it was, in all its glory, sitting in the center of the coffee table. Still fresh looking, with the soft scent of roses seductively drifting toward her.

And she'd had no intention, right up until the

moment she'd crossed this threshold, to stop by Mike's apartment for a nightcap, especially since, for the most part, she'd hardly had any alcohol at the wedding reception.

But she felt drunk anyway.

Or at least, very light-headed. But, in all honesty, that had everything to do with the moment and nothing at all to do with the frosted glass of vodka and orange juice she now held—clutched actually—in her hand.

Natalya couldn't shake the feeling that she was waiting for something to happen. Had been waiting for something to happen from the moment she'd first seen Mike walking up to her in the police station.

Get a grip, Nat.

This couldn't go anywhere, she told herself silently. She knew that. He wanted children. A legion of them eventually. He'd told her so today while they were dancing, and she'd gone cold inside then. Cold even though she wanted children, too. Wanted enough to populate a small village. The difference was that Mike *could* have children of his own if he wound up marrying someone else. She couldn't have children of her own no matter whom she married. Not unless she adopted them. She knew that wasn't what Mike had in mind. A man like Mike wanted to see his features imprinted on rambunctious miniatures.

Taking another long sip of her drink she tried to wash away her thoughts, she hadn't told him that she'd been robbed of having babies because of complications from an illness. And why should she? she mused cynically. The man didn't want medical babble, he wanted kids.

And that, ladies and gentlemen, she thought sullenly, was a deal breaker.

In her heart, Natalya knew that the minute he started talking about having kids in the future, she should have said something. But that would have made it seem as if she were assuming things between them would get serious. Serious enough where something like not being able to have babies mattered.

All that meant, she silently insisted, was that they couldn't get serious.

God, but she wanted to get serious. Badly.

Natalya took another very long sip of her drink, vaguely aware of the way the liquid coursed through her veins.

Mike sat down beside her on the sofa, the sides of his jacket hanging open, his tie undone. He looked slightly messy and she wanted to run her fingers through his hair. Wanted him to leave his imprint on her soul.

Wanted not to think, but to feel.

To feel something other than lonely, she realized. Because despite the upbeat temperament she'd been born with, she somehow felt incredibly lonely right now.

Things were changing and she'd never been a fan of change. But Clancy was dead and Sasha was married and life moved on.

This was why she needed to work so much especially lately. So that these sad, isolating thoughts couldn't find her, couldn't make her feel like this.

Maybe she shouldn't be drinking, she thought abruptly, looking accusingly at the glass in her hand. The screwdriver was almost gone. How had that happened? She'd only taken a sip. Maybe two.

Mike studied her face for a moment, moving aside the bangs that had fallen into her eyes. "What's wrong, Natalya?"

She liked the way he said her name. Halfway between the way her sisters said it and "Natalie" as if he couldn't decide where to put the accent. It was sweet.

Natalya shook her head. "Nothing."

It didn't look like nothing. She looked pensive.

"Having second thoughts about coming here?" Taking the glass from her hand, he placed it on the coffee table, next to his. Right in front of the wedding bouquet. "I could take you home." He didn't want her here against her will, or because something she'd imbibed had impaired her judgment. He *wanted* her here because she wanted to be here.

"You did," she pointed out, a slight smile curving the corners of her mouth.

What was there about her smile that made him feel as if he were lighting up inside? "You know what I mean. I don't want you to feel uncomfortable." He looked at her for a long moment. "Or do anything that you don't want to do."

That was just the trouble. She wanted to. More than she'd ever wanted to before. Just being beside him like this made her whole body sing.

"So you're going to make me beg?" There was humor in her eyes.

He felt his gut tighten. "I wouldn't dream of it," he replied just before he framed her face between his hands pressing his lips against hers.

The kiss grew slowly, deepening by layers, until it was so intense that it threatened to incinerate them both if they weren't careful.

His kiss stole her breath away and made her want him with every fiber of her being. It had always been a matter of when this was going to happen, not if, and the longer it took to happen, the larger she knew the explosion would be once it did.

She wasn't wrong.

It felt as if every vein in her body had just been set on fire. An eagerness rushed in, overtaking her in the blink of an eye, making her want to rip his clothes from his body as well as ripping away her own.

But patience, she'd learned, had its virtues. And letting Mike undress her, coaxing the zipper down, drawing the fabric away from her flesh, was far more rewarding than doing it herself.

Each time his hand passed over her, taking something else with it, or lingering to touch, to explore, to caress, it was harder and harder to breathe. Harder and harder not to just let her knees dissolve, the way they wanted to. She found herself holding on to him just to remain upright. Until that position was no longer necessary.

Desire had lit a match that had turned into a torch. He'd meant to go slow. To savor and enjoy. She wasn't his first woman, or even his tenth, but there was no doubt in his mind that she was special, even more than all the other women he'd enjoyed. From the moment he'd first kissed her, he knew there was something about this woman with flame-colored hair and flashing green eyes that set her apart.

Which was why this had been longer in coming than was his habit. In his own way, he'd been afraid of her, afraid of the way he felt around her. Afraid of the degree with which he wanted her.

The longer he waited, the more he wanted, the more he feared. This one counted. Not like

Brenda, who he'd talked himself into thinking he could marry. Natalya *really* counted.

Even as he made love to every part of her, it felt, very oddly, like his first time. Not with her but with anyone. It wasn't as if he didn't know what to expect, and yet, with Natalya, he wasn't entirely sure. He certainly had never felt as if losing control was just half a heartbeat away.

Natalya made his head spin, his blood surge and desire throb within every single part of him. Every kiss, every taste, just served to heighten his excitement.

She was an eager lover. When she pressed her naked, hot body against his, he'd almost thrown her down on the sofa and taken her right then and there. But he knew the worth of slow progress, both for her and for himself. He thrived on her pleasure, so he wanted to make sure that it was at its highest peak before they came together for the ultimate consummation.

For the first time that he could remember, control was all but elusive. It was as if he was being controlled by some unseen force, or-chestrating every sensual, blood-pounding movement.

He wanted to lose himself within her. Within the taste, the feel, the scent of her, not just within her body.

Things were happening that she'd never felt before, couldn't begin to describe to herself. A frantic need, a desire that was larger than anything she'd ever experienced before had seized her, taken control and made her prisoner the moment he'd touched his lips to hers.

She didn't know, couldn't analyze, what was happening to her. All that mattered was making love with this man. Nothing else, just here, just now. She felt like if it didn't happen, if they couldn't come together, she would expire. Disappear completely from existence.

His lips were everywhere, causing ripples that turned into tidal waves along her throat, the side of her neck, the length of her torso down to her belly and then her thighs.

And beyond.

She twisted and turned, trying to capture more, trying to flee because the enormity of what she was feeling was so overwhelming, she had no idea how to deal with it. *Sweet agony*. The term throbbed in her brain. It was the only one that seemed to fit.

Unwilling to feel this measure of excitement alone, Natalya suddenly sat up, taking his face between her hands the way he'd done earlier with hers. She gently brought him back up to her so that she could cover his mouth with her own. So that she could kiss him over and over again, the way he had her, and make him as mindless as he'd succeeded in making her.

She heard him moan. The sound utterly inflamed her.

Their bodies tangled together until they became one entity, until there was no beginning, no end, just one whole.

Sheathed deep within her, Mike began to move with an urgency he had no control over. Raising her hips, she echoed each thrust, moving with it. Together they took each other where they both needed to go. To the very top of this feeling. To have it explode within them and then have it wrap its fading wings around them as it brought them, more swiftly than they desired, back to earth.

Mike lay there beside her, watching her chest rise and fall. Listening as the sound of both their breathing mingled until it seemed as if it were just a single sound. A single breath.

His arm was beneath her and he drew her closer to him.

"Hell of a nightcap," he managed to say. But even that made him want to gasp for air. He couldn't seem to draw enough of it into his lungs. She'd depleted everything. His energy, his breath. His very mind.

"My thoughts exactly," she responded, then struggled into a semisitting position, leaning one arm across his chest, her hair flowing along it so that any movement of her head tickled his body.

He found it incredibly seductive and marveled at how he could feel anything at all after going numb just now. He felt completely drained....

And yet, something was whispering on the outer perimeter of his consciousness. Something that was trying to draw him in again.

The woman wasn't a doctor, she was a witch, he decided.

Mike began to toy with the ends of her hair, wrapping them around his finger. Thinking silly, disjointed thoughts. "So, what's a nice girl like you doing in a place like this?"

She moved her head so that she could look directly into his eyes. The look took him prisoner all over again. If he'd thought, even for a moment, that he had the upper hand here, he was deluding himself.

He was vaguely aware that it was the first time he hadn't wanted to retain complete control, the way he did over every situation he came across, and that losing it didn't even bother him the way he would have thought that it would.

She'd turned the whole world on its ear. Logic, what was left of it, told him to pick up and run. This woman could and would be trouble.

Trouble had never looked so attractive or compelling. He remained where he was, silently wishing that it could remain like this for them indefinitely. With no consequences looming on the horizon.

"Having the time of my life," Natalya finally answered, watching his expression carefully. "Or is that being too honest?" Sometimes, she knew, when you put all your cards on the table, it scared the other player away. But she'd never believed in playing games. And, until just now, the outcome of her bluntness had never mattered.

Now it did.

So she held her breath and watched him. And felt relieved when he smiled and told her that "Honesty can be very sexy."

"Can be," she repeated, not taking anything for granted. He'd begun to strum his fingers along her abdomen, making all the muscles

tighten like the strings of newly tuned harp.
Her eyes remained on his. If he lied, she'd
know. "Is it now?"

His eyes remained holding hers. He made no
effort to look away. "What do you think?"

She moved her torso in a little closer, so that
it was partially over his. A grin blossomed on
her lips as she felt him growing. Felt the
physical evidence of his resurrected desire.

It created havoc within her own core, making
her want to do it all over again. Make love
with him all night long if her stamina held.

Natalya feathered her fingertips along his
lips. "I think that the word *encore* was created
to cover moments just like this."

"Wasn't a moment," he corrected, pretending
to look serious, or as serious as he could manage.
"Was a hell of a lot longer than a moment."

Her grin turned wicked, although she was

trying to appear innocent. "I'm afraid that you're going to have to show me again. I seem to find myself temporarily suffering from amnesia."

He laughed, then suddenly shifted positions and she found herself flat on her back with Mike directly over her. His body was sealed against hers. It took everything she had not to let a moan of anticipation escape her lips.

"It's a dirty job," he told her, linking his hands with hers, his eyes holding her prisoner, "but I guess someone has to do it."

"Dirty job?" she echoed, pretending, unsuccessfully, to take offense.

"You heard me."

That wasn't all she heard.

She also heard bells—loud ones. And for once, they weren't coming from either her cell phone or his. They were coming from inside of her.

Natalya wrapped her arms around his neck and gladly gave herself up to the sensations that had already taken hold of her.

She'd had every intention of going back to her apartment before midnight.

And then before dawn.

But somehow, it didn't happen. Neither of them wanted to initiate the first step that would ultimately separate them, taking them away from this rare moment, this rare place they'd discovered. Both feared in their hearts that something precisely like this might never happen again, or at least, not to this degree. And there were no disturbances. No babies suddenly in need of attention, no sad souls who had left the world abruptly, no mystery needing Mike's exclusive attention. For once, there was nothing to interrupt the evening.

But paradise could only continue for so long. With first light came reality, seeking to reestablish its claim on them both.

Natalya opened her eyes with enormous reluctance. The second that she did, she found Mike leaning over her, his head propped up on his upturned hand as he looked down at her.

God, she had to look awful. But she couldn't very well throw the blanket over her head. He'd already seen her. "What are you doing?"

Enjoying himself, he thought. "Watching you sleep."

"Why?" She tried to be glib, to hide the awkwardness she felt. Belatedly, she realized that she hadn't pulled the cover over her body. She tugged it into place now. "Am I doing something entertaining?"

"Not now." He curbed the urge to pull the blanket away again. "But you were."

She stared at him, almost afraid of the answer. "In my sleep?"

"No, before that." He threaded his arm around her waist, tucking her against his side. "Anyone ever tell you that you are one exciting lady?"

God, but this felt right. She knew she should be getting up, should be creating her own space again, but all she wanted to do was be with him a little longer.

"Not that I recall."

"Well, you are." If he didn't get up now, he was going to start making love to her all over again and he wasn't sure how she'd respond to that in the light of day. Mornings had a way of changing the rules of the game. "Want me to make you breakfast?"

Her eyes widened as she looked up at him. "You cook, too?"

He lifted a single shoulder, then let it fall again. "Passably."

"Only passably?" He nodded. She wasn't hungry for anything that could be placed on a plate. But she did want something that he could serve up, hot and ready. Oh, God, she was thinking like a guy and she didn't even care. "How about we end this on a high note?"

He settled his body against hers, reading between the lines but wanting to be absolutely sure the text wasn't just wishful thinking. "What do you mean?"

She raised her arms to his. "Guess."

With a laugh, he took her into his arms. "How many guesses do I get?"

Her body was already humming in anticipation as she felt the warmth of him radiating through the blanket. "I'll be very disappointed if it takes you more than one to get the answer."

"Then I'd better not disappoint you."

Chapter 12

Natalya put her key in the lock and turned it softly. Her hand on the doorknob, she moved it a fraction of an inch at a time. Taking a deep breath, she entered the apartment on tiptoes, carrying her shoes in her hand.

Only to find herself looking straight into Kady's amused eyes.

Her sister looked as if she were on her way out. Just her luck. "Welcome home, Cinderella. Is the ball over?" Kady guessed, not bothering to hide her wide grin.

Natalya pressed her lips together. She'd been hoping to slip in without making Kady aware of the time. The very last thing she wanted right now were questions, especially since she couldn't begin to honestly answer any of her own, beginning with *What the hell was she doing?*

She had no idea what she was doing, getting in deeper with a man she couldn't possibly have a future with. But the truth of it was, the more she was with Mike, the more she wanted to be with him. And at least part of her felt that he felt the same way, as well. Which made it all the better, even as it made the situation worse.

Natalya held her hand up to ward off anything that might be coming from her younger sister. "Please, no third degree, Kady."

"Third?" Kady echoed. "Honey, that wasn't even first degree. I was just a little worried about you, that's all. And a little envious," she added with a wink. "He is a hunk."

Natalya tried her best to be nonchalant. The half shrug was careless. "He's okay."

This time Kady hooted. "Okay?" She slipped her arm around Natalya's shoulders. "Sweetie, I have *never* known you to spend your time with just plain 'okay.' You're not the type, no matter what you want Mama and Dad to think." It was a valiant fight, but her resolve to keep her questions to herself died a quick death. She *had* to ask. "Is it serious?"

Natalya threw off her wrap and let her clutch purse drop on top of it. "No. Yes." She held her head, which was beginning to ache. "I don't know."

Unfazed, Kady nodded. "Fair enough." She

slanted a look at Natalya's face. "So, do you want it to be serious?"

On occasion, she'd hedge to her sisters, but she never once lied outright. "Yes, but it can't."

Clear as mud, Kady thought. It *had* to be love. Out loud, she said cheerfully, "I love riddles. Do I get any more clues?"

She might as well tell Kady everything, Natalya thought. "Mike wants children."

Kady looked as if she were still waiting to hear what the problem was. "So?"

Had it slipped Kady's mind? "I can't have any, remember?" Natalya told her.

To which Kady could only shake her head as her sister took hold of her arms to keep her from walking away. "Nat, Nat, Nat, you're a doctor. You of all people should know that there are *so* many options available to us these days." She paused for only a moment. "Not the least of which is adoption."

Natalya didn't think that was an option in this case. "I think Mike wants his own." The words came out with a sigh.

Kady peered up at her face, searching it. "You think or you know?"

Restless, upset and on the verge on being emotional Natalya threw up her hands and began to move away. "I couldn't exactly interrogate him about it."

"Number one, when you adopt, the child instantly 'becomes' your own. Number two, there're so many ways to have a baby these days that didn't exist a generation ago. I read about this woman who couldn't give birth to a baby so her mother volunteered to carry it to term for her. She wound up having twins."

Natalya laughed. "Now there's something to

ask Mama for Christmas. 'Could you give birth to your grandchild, Mama?' Provided she could, of course, which we both know isn't possible anymore."

Kady refused to be put off. She did, however, come close to losing her temper. She couldn't remember ever seeing her sister like this. This Mike person had her twisted up inside. Whether that was good or not remained to be seen.

"Stop putting obstacles in your way, Nat. Let nature take its course." She peered closer, and then grinned. "Although—" she used her thumb to gently wipe away a slight smudge of lipstick from her sister's mouth "—I think you've already started on that path." She looked at her meaningfully.

Natalya picked up her purse and began to head for her room. "I've got to go change."

"Highly recommended," Kady called after her. "I'll see you later. I've got to go see a patient."

House calls were a thing of the past, but Natalya knew for a fact that there was one patient, a man in his late seventies, that Kady indulged. She turned around to look at Kady.

"Today?"

Kady lifted one shoulder and let it drop. "Hey, hearts don't look at calendars." Hand on the doorknob, she paused one last time. "You going to be all right?"

"Sure." Natalya tried to sound as cheerful, and positive, as possible. But even as she said it, turning toward her room, she knew she wasn't. Not for a while, at least. Not until she could get everything sorted out in her mind.

An hour later found her no better. She needed air. Needed to go out and try to clear her head. It was Sunday. She always liked Sundays in New York. The traffic, both pedestrian and automobile, was far less congested on a Sunday. The office buildings stood like tall, silent sentries. It made walking less of a competitive sport and allowed her to window-shop. Window-shopping was her favorite diversion. And for once, it was one of those wonderful sunny days that came along so rarely in New York.

Her mind made up, she took her jacket out of the closet and put it on. As she began to walk out of the apartment, Natalya absently put her hand into her pocket. And stopped dead.

Her fingers came in contact with something. It took her only a second to recognize the thin, smooth shape. It was a camera.

Clancy's camera.

She'd forgotten all about it. Taking it out, she closed the door again and stared at the slim object in her hand. It hardly looked like a camera. For as long as she could remember, Clancy had always been into electronic gadgets. Be it a computer, a cell phone or a camera, he liked them cutting-edge fast, and the tinier, the better. And this was almost spylike tiny.

A pang zigzagged over her heart. For a moment, Natalya debated just putting the camera away again until she could deal with looking at the photographs a little better.

But then she suddenly thought, what if Clancy had managed to take a photo of his killer? Or, at the very least, a photo of the last person he'd been with the night he died. That could help reconstruct his evening. So far, it seemed as if nobody had seen him from the time he left the mortuary until the time he turned up behind the art gallery. She knew he both date and time stamped everything, it was part of his obsession with organization.

Natalya took a deep breath and pressed the view menu on the camera. One by one, she began going through the photographs on the memory card backward to the most recent. There was nothing remarkable about the first few. It was almost as if he'd snapped them in the shadows. But then, that was Clancy. It seemed almost ironic to her that, with his passion for cameras, he'd never actually taken the time to learn how to frame scenes to their best advantage.

She'd gone through five shots of shadows and was about to stop when she saw the photograph. The light was bright, making everything visible. It had obviously been taken at the funeral parlor.

Natalya cringed. The photograph was of a

dead man. He looked to be somewhere in his thirties. By his build, he appeared to be in the prime of his life.

The man was stark naked.

"Oh, God, Clancy, was that snake, Tolliver, right? Were you doing something with those dead people you weren't supposed to?" She could feel tears gathering in her eyes. There had to be some mistake. Clancy wasn't like that. He *wasn't.*

How well do we know anyone?

The question echoed in her head as she moved back to the next photo and then the one that had been taken before that. When she came to her sixth shot, her stomach had completely turned. What the director had said about Clancy had to be right. He'd been doing improper things with the bodies that were brought into the funeral parlor to be prepared for burial.

She almost stopped, but then, she'd come this far, she might as well see it through.

Natalya's breath lodged in her throat when she saw the seventh shot. It was of a woman.

Something was wrong here. Clancy was not in to women, he admitted that to her when they were thirteen.

But if he wasn't into women, why had he taken the photograph? It didn't make sense.

She needed to see things more clearly than the tiny screen allowed. Camera in hand, she went back to her room and switched on her computer, then waited for it to go through its paces. It moaned and groaned and emitted a battery of strange noises, its lights winking and flashing.

"C'mon, c'mon," she urged impatiently.

Once the noises and lights had settled down, she slipped the memory card out of the camera and into a slot on her tower. Within a minute, she was pulling up the shot of the nude woman, enlarging it until it filled her entire monitor.

She caught her breath as she saw what Clancy had seen. Quickly, she flipped to the other photos, viewing them one by one.

It was beginning to make sense.

Natalya never bothered shutting off her color printer. It took far too long to come around when she needed it. She hit Print and the machine came out of sleep mode. It was printing within seconds. Slowly, eight by tens of Clancy's photographs began to emerge from the mouth of the printer. Mike was going to need to see these.

Mike hadn't known exactly what to make of her phone call when it came. Essentially, Natalya'd said nothing, only that she needed to see him right away. With the scent of her body still fresh in his head, not to mention on his sheets, he could only think that she was returning because she wanted more of the same.

Well, that made two of them, he thought.

He'd begged off from his mother's weekly Sunday lunch and was glad now that he had. Otherwise, he might have missed Natalya's call.

Again, it bothered him a little that the moment he'd told her to come over, he caught himself looking forward to her appearance with an anticipation that he wasn't accustomed to. Now, all that mattered was that she was coming over.

Replaying her last words in his head, he realized that she'd sounded mysterious, but, hell, that was her right. He had to admit, it kind of made things more interesting.

Maybe, he thought, as he went to answer the

door, she was having as much trouble reconciling everything that had happened last night as he did. Like where, if anywhere, was this going?

No point in wondering about that until it got to the starting gate, right? It seemed like a solid philosophy. He still went on wondering.

When Mike opened the door, she was wearing a blue sweater beneath a jacket and a pair of jeans that looked as if they'd been applied with a paintbrush. He could feel his temperature rising already.

"Hi."

"Hi." She sounded breathless, as if she'd been running. Or wrestling emotionally with something, unsure of which side to take.

Damn, he had to stop overanalyzing things.

Mike laughed at himself as he closed the door behind her. He was a cop. Overanalyzing was what he did for a living.

"Elevator out again?" he asked. When she looked at him quizzically, he added, "You seem breathless."

"No, it's working," she assured him, trying to measure out every word. She certainly didn't want him to think she was panting at the very sight of him—although it would take very little for that to happen. He'd answered the door shirtless.

"I didn't expect to see you again so soon," he confessed.

The remark stopped her for a second. Was that his way of saying that Saturday night—or was that Sunday morning—had just been one of those things? Great, but over?

Stop it, Nat. This is bigger than your all-consuming attraction to Supercop. This is about Clancy and what he was getting ready to tell you.

"I have something to show you," she told him. She held up the manila envelope she'd brought.

"All right," Mike said gamely, his curiosity aroused. "Come into the living room. The lighting's better there."

Natalya shrugged out of her leather jacket as she went. When she felt his hands behind her, she sucked in her breath, surprised, before she regained control. Looking a little amused at her reaction, Mike took the jacket from her.

She realized that her fingers were shaking slightly as she opened the manila envelope and took out the photographs she'd printed less than an hour ago. She handed him the lot.

"Here."

Slightly bewildered, Mike took the photographs from her. The bewilderment grew as he looked at the first photograph and then the second.

"You came here to show me naked pictures of men?" He raised his eyes to hers, his expression a little uncertain. "I don't—"

"The pictures are from Clancy's camera. He took them."

He continued to go through the photographs. He dealt with death every day, but this was a little hard to stomach. "We didn't find a camera."

She debated making up an excuse, then decided that if he pressed her, the truth would come out. And then he wouldn't know when to believe her. It was best to face the music now and get it over with.

She slid the tip of her tongue along her lips before beginning. "That's because that first day, when you came into the apartment, you startled me. I was holding the camera and I guess I must have slipped it into my pocket without realizing it. It's practically the size of a credit card," she added quickly, "and with everything else going on, I guess I just forgot about it. Until this morning." She bit her lower lip before concluding. "I put my jacket on and there it was."

Finished, he straightened the photographs in his hands and looked at her. "Okay, I still don't see—"

That's because he didn't know what he was looking for, she thought. And because he hadn't looked at them through eyes that were desperate to absolve a friend. "The photographs are of some of the people who were brought in to the mortuary."

He inclined his head. "That would account for the pale complexions, but—"

"No, look," she ordered tersely. To underscore what she meant, she pointed to the photograph on top. To the scar that was visible. "See?"

"What is it I'm seeing?" But even as he asked, he realized what she was pointing out. "Those are incisions." Just like the ones on the bodies of the homeless victims. Quickly, he went through the rest of the photographs again. Different people, same discovery. "Those are all incisions."

She nodded her head vigorously. "Yes. And they all appear fresh."

"How can you tell?"

She traced one line. "The scarring hadn't begun. Because the person was dead."

He felt a stirring in his stomach. The same kind he felt when he was onto something. But he wanted to be absolutely sure of what little facts there were. "And these were on your friend's camera?"

"Yes." Excitement vibrated in her voice. "I think this is what Clancy meant when he said he was onto something. It wasn't anything to do with falsifying the bookkeeping. This is a whole lot bigger than that." Her eyes widened as her voice gained momentum. "Those incisions are in the region of the kidneys. It's too much of a coincidence."

Mike was trying to wrap his head around what this could mean. "You think people are being killed for their organs?"

She didn't know if she would go that far, but it definitely had something to do with organ theft. "Or at least having organs harvested just after they died. There were no autopsies done." That was evident because of the lack of wide, V-shaped incisions across the breast plate. "These people died and were hustled to the mortuary, as per instruction by whoever was overseeing their arrangements. But before they got there, someone decided to make them a little lighter. And their own pockets a little heavier."

"Someone like a surgeon." It wasn't really a question. The incisions he was looking at had all been closed neatly, with perfect stitching, as if to make the lines all but invisible.

"Had to be," she agreed. "Those incisions are too good. And someone had to know what they were doing, otherwise, the organ would be butchered and useless. Timing is everything in these cases." She took a breath. There was an ache in the center of her chest. "Clancy stumbled onto this and they killed him for it," she concluded.

"It looks that way," he agreed. Carefully, he returned the photographs to their envelope. "But we can't know for sure."

She looked at him, stunned. "You've got the photographs. What more do you need?"

"The actual bodies, for starters." He knew she wouldn't like hearing that, because it sounded as if he didn't believe what she was saying. But she didn't understand how carefully a case had to be made. "We need to have autopsies done in order to make sure that these bodies are missing organs before we start to point fingers."

He was talking about exhumation. "Are you going to go to the next of kin?" she asked him.

It wasn't that simple. "In my experience, most next of kin really don't want the body of their loved one disturbed. They'd rather close their eyes and try to move on."

"If someone I loved had been violated like that, I'd want to know so that I could make whoever was responsible pay," she declared with feeling.

She was one hell of a fiery woman. He

liked her spirit. But that still didn't make the case for them.

"'Ignorance is bliss' isn't just something printed on a dish towel. Most people would rather not hear things that'll give them nightmares."

Well, she couldn't argue with that. "So what are you going to do?"

What he always did as a backup plan. "Get to the D.A.'s office. If I show him these photographs and tell him what we think is going on, he might be able to come up with the name of a friendly judge who doesn't mind disturbing the dead."

She nodded, then said something she hoped might help him persuade the D.A. "This might tie into the case where those homeless men were killed in the park." He looked at her, surprised. "I read the newspaper on occasion."

"It might tie in with that." He didn't bother telling her that he'd already thought that. Why steal her thunder? He grabbed his jacket from the hook where he'd hung it. He knew where the D.A. lived and these wouldn't keep until tomorrow. "Thanks for bringing these."

She read between the lines. He was planning on leaving her behind. "Thank me later. I'm coming with you."

The hell she was. "Stay here and wait for me," he instructed.

She placed her hand on the envelope. "They're my photos."

He wasn't about to be put over a barrel. "How do you figure that?"

She continued to hold on to the corner of the envelope. "Clancy left me all his worldly goods. Last time I looked, a camera was a worldly good." She smiled. "Want to waste time, arguing with me? My mother says I'm very stubborn. It's a trait all Polish women share and if she thinks I'm very stubborn—"

He had no doubt that Natalya was probably capable of arguing until hell produced a skating rink for penguins. "C'mon." He sighed, handing her her jacket.

She grinned, preceding him out the door. "Knew you'd see it my way."

Chapter 13

District Attorney Hayden Sommerville looked less than enthusiastic about finding a police detective standing on the doorstep of his Staten Island home on a Sunday afternoon.

Tall, with a full head of prematurely silver-gray hair, Sommerville looked more like Hollywood's version of a leading man than the sharp legal mind that he was. His good looks, coupled with his flamboyant style, had gotten him more than his share of press coverage and women. The latter, so the story went, was a thing of the past now that he had finally settled down. He had two children under the age of six, both of whom had more energy than an entire battalion of kindergarteners.

The children, Nathan and Jake, were currently trying to poke their way around their father's imposing body and across the front door threshold in order to see what was going on. But Sommerville stood like an iron statue, refusing to let them out.

It looked to Natalya as if the man was fighting a battle with his temper and was in serious in danger of losing it.

"It's Sunday, Detective," Sommerville pointed out, enunciating each word as if it were to stand alone. "A day of rest and a day that I promised to my family." He looked at Mike meaningfully, lowering his voice so that it carried no farther than the front step. "Cut me a break, DiPalma. I am half a business phone call away from a divorce right now. My wife said that if I didn't give her and the boys some time alone, I wouldn't *have* her and the boys."

Despite some posturing, Sommerville was one of the good guys. Mike could more than sympathize with the man. But he also knew that they could very well be fighting time. If Tolliver was somehow involved in a black market scheme to sell organs, there was nothing to prevent the funeral director from fleeing before they could arrest him. And until they had some definite proof to show the police department, their hands were tied.

"Mr. Sommerville," Mike began respectfully, "I wouldn't be here if it wasn't important."

"My marriage is important," the D.A.

replied tersely. One hand behind him, Sommerville urged his sons back into the living room as he began to close the door to his Colonial-style home.

"This is connected to the homeless men who were killed in the park recently," Natalya managed to blurt out before the door shut. "The case that the mayor's so interested in," she added quickly.

The door stopped closing. After a beat, Sommerville pushed it open a little wider. His dark blue eyes took closer measure of her. "And you are?"

"Dr. Natalya Pulaski." Counting this as a victory, she put her hand out.

Instead of taking it, Sommerville looked down at her face. His expression was utterly unreadable. There was no emotion in his voice.

"All right, you have my attention." He turned

his head slightly so that his voice could carry. His sons were ready to launch a second assault on the door. "Boys, go play video games."

"Really?" Jake, the oldest, exclaimed gleefully.

"Really." Not wasting any further words on a debate, the D.A. eased himself out of the house, closing the door firmly behind him. "Their mother saves that for special occasions. It helps to have a secret weapon." He sobered, but there was interest in his eyes. "All right, talk fast."

The man didn't know what he was leaving himself open for, Mike thought, amused despite the gravity of the situation. He wasn't wrong. Even as he began to explain the reason for their unscheduled visit, Natalya was interjecting her words into his narrative. He decided to retreat and leave the explaining to her, seeing as how it was the hunt for her friend that had initiated all this in the first place. Besides, even though she talked fast, every word was clear as a bell, not an easy feat in his book.

In the space of less than five minutes, the D.A. was up to speed. In ten, he promised to get the wheels moving for the court order that they had come seeking. And then, he was advising them to leave. Quickly.

The next moment, he'd disappeared into the house again.

"Well, that went well. We got him to say yes and his wife isn't divorcing him," Natalya commented as she followed Mike back to his motorcycle.

Mike caught himself laughing. He'd known Sommerville in his much-lauded bachelor days. Now, the six-foot-five D.A. was wrapped around the finger of a dark-haired woman who barely came up to five-one. How the mighty have fallen.

"That we know of," he underscored. "He might still be in hot water. In my experience, women have a sixth sense about these things."

Natalya frowned. She wasn't entirely following him. "What things?"

"Lines being crossed that they've drawn in the sand." The D.A. didn't look like the type to be kept on a short leash, but looks in this case were deceiving. He saw amusement filtering across Natalya's face, but he'd be willing to believe it was for a different reason.

"Had a lot of experience with that, have you?"

In an attempt to divert her attention, he smiled seductively at her.

"A gentleman never elaborates." Reaching inside the saddlebag, he took out the spare helmet and handed it to her. "I doubt if that court order is going to come through before tomorrow at the earliest." He deliberately let his eyes slide over her from head to foot. "What do you suggest we do with the rest of the day?"

Desire rippled through her body, taking parts of her prisoner. Scenes from last night and this morning replayed themselves in her mind, adding fuel.

Fastening the helmet, Natalya got on behind him. Secure, she tucked her arms around his waist. It took effort not to lean her cheek against his back. "I'll leave that up to you," she told him.

"I was hoping you'd say that." With a laugh, he knocked away the kickstand. The next moment, they roared back into the street.

This wasn't like her.

There were articles in at least the last three medical journals she'd promised herself to get to this afternoon. And there was a stack of charts she'd been meaning to annotate before having Vicki file them away. She'd had every intention of going into her office in the late afternoon to catch up on things that always seemed to get out of hand during the week. This seemed like an excellent time for it inasmuch as she had no small patients in the hospital to look in on.

So what was she doing, lying here in bed beside this man, dressed in nothing more than a smile, a smile that seemed to have a life of its own? She had no excuse, no explanation.

What she had was this overwhelming desire that refused to be quenched, refused to be sated. The only thing it seemed capable of doing was growing and it was doing that at a breathtaking rate.

This was only making it harder on her, she

argued silently, even as her body turned into his, harder to endure the inevitable when it happened. She'd never been one who stubbornly clung to a habit, never allowed herself to gain an addiction to anyone or anything. Nothing had ever had control over her. And yet, here she was, being led around by her emotions, her desires, and not trying to do a damn thing to save herself.

Natalya propped herself up on her elbow. Pushing her hair out of her eyes, she looked down at him.

"You know, Detective, we have to stop meeting like this," she quipped.

"Why?" There was humor in his eyes. "Works for me." And then he looked at her more closely. Something he saw in her face had him backtracking. "You're serious, aren't you?"

Back to the yes-no tug of war, she thought.

There was no point in trying to be evasive about it. "What I am is confused."

He tried to tease her out of it. "What you are," he contradicted, "is magnificent." Cupping the back of her head, Mike gently brought her face down to his and kissed her. The kiss worked itself into his system, spilling out through his veins like maple syrup in July. Sweet. Delectable. "We both overthink things," he told her after a beat. "Maybe for once, we should just let whatever happens happen."

If only. But she had been raised to believe that every action had a consequence. And the consequences of what she was allowing herself to do here with him were extremely steep. "That's not very responsible," she pointed out.

His response surprised her. "Maybe I don't always want to be a grown-up." He slid his finger along her collarbone. "I'm a grown-up on the job. In my private life…" He let his voice trail off. His smile alone was enough to make her blood sizzle.

It took effort to rein herself in. Effort not to just throw him flat on his back and have her way with him. Damn, but he had turned her into a completely different person. "Is that where all those women come in?"

His expression was innocence personified. "What women?"

"The ones you said you had all that experience with," she reminded him.

He shook his head. "That's *not* what I said." And definitely not what he wanted her to think. The women who had come before her had begun to blur the first time he kissed her. And had all but faded from memory the moment they'd made love. "Is that what you want to do with the rest of this afternoon?" He underscored the question by pressing a kiss to the side of her neck. It was followed by another. "Talk?"

Heat was springing up, taking hold. Clouding her brain. "Talking is good," she managed to get out thickly, already losing the battle she hadn't really believed she could win. He was touching her, caressing her. Making her crazy.

"This is better," he countered, raising her hair from her neck so that he could kiss that side, as well.

She was dissolving right in front of him, she thought. Any willpower she'd hoped to summon had dashed away like a newly freed deserter. Her limbs felt heavy, languid. "You don't play fair," she protested.

"Never said I wanted to be fair." His breath feathered along her skin as it preceded his lips.

She could feel herself melting and heating at the very same moment. If she'd been a candle, she'd have long been nothing more than just a puddle of color.

"No," she acknowledged hoarsely, her voice barely above a whisper, "that you didn't."

Okay, tomorrow she'd tell him. Tomorrow. Monday, when things began fresh for the week. When everything moved along at a faster clip. Tomorrow she'd find a way to let him know that she couldn't have children. And then, the next move would be his.

Now was for enjoying this wild, wonderful feeling that he created, for savoring it as she struggled to keep from falling over the brink into an abyss.

With effort, she turned her body into his and began to strum her fingers along his torso, her tempo increasing as needs and wants hammered through her, growing ever more frenzied. When she touched him intimately, she heard his sharp intake of breath, felt his desire for her surge. She would have laughed in triumph if she'd had the strength for that. She was saving what little was left of her strength for the ultimate culmination and joining. That would make the third time in as many hours.

Whatever regrets she felt were waiting to pounce on her she managed to keep in abeyance. All she wanted in this moment was to be his and to pretend that this wonderful sensation could last.

Tempted to stay the night again, Natalya forced herself to return to her apartment. He insisted on bringing her back. It was late, he'd reminded her, and the city that never slept wasn't always as savory as everyone would have wanted it to be.

She came in so late, she was able to get to her own room without encountering Kady or any of Kady's knowing looks. The following morning, still yawning, she quickly got ready, pausing only for a moment when she went to select her underwear from the drawer. The colors were still together, but the types—sexy, functional—were not. Kady, she thought. It had to have been Kady, rummaging for something sensual to put on. She was going to have ask her about it when she got the chance.

It wasn't far to her office and she decided to walk instead of taking the bus or her car. She was hoping to walk off some of the excess tension that was vibrating through her.

For once, her schedule wasn't full. There was a large break between her first two appointments and her third one, a highly unusual occurrence. Especially on a Monday when parents who'd spent the entire weekend debating whether or not those sniffles their child was exhibiting were actually a sign of something more serious called.

Sitting at her desk with that same stack of files that she'd neglected yesterday, Natalya drummed her fingers on her desk. She hadn't heard from Mike yet, which could mean that he hadn't heard from the D.A. Or, she supposed it could just mean that he was too busy to call. It wasn't as if he had nothing else to do. Cases came in, right and left, hardly leaving any time for him to breathe.

Still, you'd think, because they had a special connection…

Natalya stopped herself. She had to remember that she couldn't expect too much from Mike, other than a good time. And even that was finite. To expect more was leaving herself open to disappointment. A man like Mike was faithful to the moment. When it left, so would he.

She forced herself to think of something else, which brought her mind back around to Clancy and the photographs. While they were waiting for the court order, Mike had told her that he was going to look into putting names to those bodies.

Maybe, she suddenly thought, she should be looking in to where they came from. Ellis Brothers handled funeral arrangements for people from all the five boroughs, not to mention the hospitals in the area that shipped their nameless dead to them. She didn't have the time to contact all the hospitals, but at the very least, she could explore one avenue.

Patience Memorial sent their unclaimed deceased to Ellis Brothers with the county footing the bill.

Were any of those people in the photographs Clancy took from Patience Memorial?

Her head began to ache. She needed answers to questions she hadn't completely formed yet. Rummaging around in her middle drawer, she found a bottle of aspirin. Natalya swallowed it dry, then reached for the telephone on her desk. She had to start somewhere.

It took her over an hour, with so many transfers and lost connections, but she finally had a name. The doctor who was in charge of handing off the bodies of the unclaimed John and Jane Does was Dr. Ralph Jessop. Funny that Clancy had never mentioned him by name, although he had grumbled several times about "the pompous ass" he'd had to deal with at P.M. Still, being a pompous ass didn't immediately mean that a person was capable of breaking the law.

She'd seen Jessop around, even exchanged a few words with him once at one of the fundraisers the hospital periodically held, but she really knew very little about the man. What she knew hadn't been flattering. Rumor had it that Jessop was a player, a wealthy man, thanks to his family, who wanted to be wealthier.

Did that automatically mean that he was willing to cut into bodies in order to excise organs that would find their way to the black market?

She didn't know. She needed to talk to Jessop, to feel him out, before she came to any sort of conclusions.

Natalya hadn't a clue what she was going to

say to the doctor when he answered his phone. His field was radiology. Maybe she could tell him that she needed his professional opinion about one of her patient's X-rays. But she had nothing outstanding to offer.

And then she remembered that Sasha once had a patient who'd required an emergency appendectomy only to discover that the pain was being caused by a cyst pressing on the organ. A very particular kind of cyst, with hair and nails all wrapped up inside it. In effect, the patient discovered that she was supposed to be conjoined twins, except that the second twin hadn't developed. That might whet Jessop's appetite—if things medical still moved him.

She knew Sasha kept the X-ray in an old box of archived files. Her sister wouldn't mind her stealing the X-ray for a good cause. Sasha's nurse, Lisa, would undoubtedly know where to locate the file....

All plans of intercepting Dr. Jessop with the unusual X-ray came to an abrupt halt for the moment. The receptionist in radiology informed her that Dr. Jessop was out for the day. The physician had taken a personal day to pay a visit to his tax accountant about setting up another SEP account.

Natalya could tell by the woman's tone what the receptionist thought about that. There was obviously no love lost between the two. Natalya had a suspicion that perhaps the good doctor rubbed more than one person the wrong way.

Still didn't make him a grave robber, so to speak. Well, she wasn't about to find out one way or another today, Natalya thought, replacing the receiver.

So near and yet so far.

She took a breath, trying to calm herself. But it was all so damn frustrating.

For a moment, Natalya thought about putting in a call to Mike to see if he'd made any progress with either the names or the court order. She had both his cell phone and his number at the precinct. She debated satisfying her curiosity at the risk of being thought of as pushy or just hanging tight.

But she was pushy, she thought. No reason to hide it.

But she never got to make the call. Vicki was knocking on her door. The next moment, the nurse peeked into the room. "Mrs. Russell is on the phone, frantic. Ryan pushed navy beans up his nose."

"Enterprising little guy," Natalya quipped. Obviously, quiet time was over. "Tell her to calm down and bring him in. And to count herself lucky that it's not pussy willow season."

Vicki laughed as she withdrew.

He needed names. The judge that Sommerville had called had granted the court order that would allow them to exhume the bodies of the people in the photographs, and only those.

The problem was, they didn't have any names. They did, however, thanks to Natalya's OCD friend, have times and dates. That narrowed down the time frame considerably. They could locate the names via Ellis Brothers' files.

That meant that he, and Louis, had to go back to Tolliver a third time. They needed the man to hand over the names of the people who had come through his doors during the time in question.

Mike knew that they were going to get an

argument from the mortuary director and that, most likely, a warrant would have to be issued. But being around Natalya had its effects. It had made him into an optimist, or at least partially so. He decided to give Tolliver the benefit of the doubt and ask him first.

"You never know," Mike theorized, using Louis as a sounding board as they drove to the mortuary, "the guy might only be guilty of having a really bad personality. The threat of scandal makes a lot of people more cooperative."

Louis stopped at the light and looked at his partner. Mike had never been on the gloomy side, but there was an odd positive bounce to his step this morning.

"You seem pretty chipper today," he commented, slanting another look at Mike. The light turned green and Louis stepped on the gas.

Mike kept his eyes on the road, even though he

wasn't driving. "Looks like we might be clearing three cases, why shouldn't I be chipper?"

But Louis shook his head. "This isn't a clearing-three-cases kind of chipper. You seeing someone new?" Even as he asked, the answer seemed to dawn on him. "That doc?" Reaching the mortuary, he eased the car into the lot behind the building. "The one with the dead friend you found? Pretty classy stuff, DiPalma." Getting out after Mike, Louis locked all four doors. He lengthened his stride to keep up and was almost skipping by the time they reached the front entrance. "Sure you're not out of your league?"

Mike walked into the building. "I'm not even going to answer that."

"You don't have to." Louis laughed shortly. "I can read you like a book."

The receptionist wasn't at her desk and

things appeared quiet in the funeral parlor. "Well, stop reading and start being a cop. It's time to flex a little muscle and scare Tolliver into cooperating."

Moving ahead of him, Louis peered into one of the viewing rooms, looking for the director. "Um, Mike, I don't think we're going to be able to do that." He turned around to look at his partner. "Looks to me like the guy's past scaring."

Or caring, Mike thought, as he walked into the room to see what Louis was talking about. There, lying in the casket that was on display, was Tolliver. Permanently, from the looks of it.

Chapter 14

Mike made his way over to the casket and placed two fingers to the side of Tolliver's neck, trying to detect a pulse. There was nothing. Frowning, he then held the same fingers just before the man's nostrils. Again, nothing.

At his side, Louis raised his eyebrows quizzically. "Is he—"

"As a doornail," Mike concluded, dropping his hand for a moment.

Louis nodded toward the man's still chest, pointing out the obvious. "He's got some kind of piece of paper on his chest."

"Gee, I would have missed that, Louis," Mike said drolly. "Seeing as how it's lying there on his chest." Mike took out a fresh pair of plastic gloves from his pocket and pulled them on before reaching for the paper.

The first thing he noticed when he unfolded it was that it was typed. Red flags went up instantly.

"'I did it.'" he read out loud. "'I killed Clancy. I'm responsible for everything and I can't take the guilt any longer.'" Mike carefully refolded the note and looked at Louis.

"Tolliver committed suicide?" Louis said skeptically, looking at the man in the casket.

Mike shook his head. "Not the type," he commented. "I can't see him climbing into the casket and then killing himself." Setting the note on top of another casket, he began to examine Tolliver's lifeless body. "No signs of struggle," he noted, more to himself than to his partner. "No stab marks, no gunshot wounds."

"Poison gets my vote," Louis volunteered. "Maybe he took some pills."

Lack of any other evidence would point to that, but from another venue, Mike thought. "Or someone gave them to him."

"You don't think it was suicide?" It wasn't really a question, but an assumption.

Louis looked around, obviously wondering the same thing Mike was. Where was everyone? It wasn't after hours, there should have been at least one attendant, besides the receptionist, yet the area was as dead as its director.

Mike picked up the note again. "Most people about to kill themselves don't usually sit down at a computer and print out their suicide note. It's too impersonal and suicide is *very* personal. They scribble something dramatic down as their final words." He indicated the note. "At a time like that, neatness isn't their main concern."

"And unless the killer's also a forger, he can't take a chance on a handwritten note because the handwriting would be different," Louis agreed. "So a printer's his only option."

Nodding, Mike handed him the paper. "Give this to forensics, see if it can be matched to one of the printers here." He was pretty certain that he'd seen at least two in Tolliver's office, a laser printer and one that printed in color.

Taking his handkerchief out, Lou placed it over two fingers and gingerly took the note from him. "So you think someone here did it?"

Mike thought of the people he had encountered on his two other visits to the mortuary. None had appeared particularly devious. "Most likely whoever killed Tolliver just used what was on hand—unless they had already printed the note before they came to see him."

Still holding the note in his handkerchief, Louis looked down and studied the dapper-looking man whose appearance had apparently meant a great deal to him. Even in death, not a hair was out of place. "Think this means that we're getting close?"

It was hard to say. "Maybe. Or maybe whoever else is involved is worried about loose ends. Or the killer found out that Tolliver was careless."

Wavy eyebrows drew together like caterpillars huddling for warmth. "Careless?"

"Natalya's friend took photographs of the dead bodies, focusing on the incisions," he reminded his partner. "I'd call that a pretty large loose end."

"Then whoever performed the 'surgeries' killed Tolliver?" Louis concluded.

"Maybe," Mike allowed. He didn't like putting all his eggs in one basket. "Or maybe the person behind this whole scheme did it."

The room was too eerie for Louis. He moved over to the wall and turned the dimmer up to its maximum wattage. "Could be one and the same," he theorized.

That was another possibility, Mike thought, nodding his head. "Could be."

Louis blew out a breath, joining him. He had a perturbed expression on his face. "Not a whole lot of concrete answers here, are there?"

"And that's why they call it detective *work,* Louis," Mike responded. He took out his cell phone and put in a call to the medical examiner's office. The irony of where he was making the call from, and for whom, was not lost on him.

* * *

"Tolliver's dead."

Those were the first words of greeting Mike said to Natalya. He'd stopped by her office to pick her up for dinner. After she had called him to find out if he'd managed to get Tolliver to open his files so that he could get the list of names he needed.

Instead of answering her, Mike had volunteered to fill her in as much as he was able to over a meal. He thought he'd detected a slight hesitation, but chalked it up to his imagination.

Frozen in midstep as she led the way to the back doors of the E.R., Natalya slowly turned around to look at him. "Dead? Somebody killed Tolliver?"

The conclusion interested him. "Now why would you ask me that? Why wouldn't you just ask if he killed himself?"

The thought of the man committing suicide never occurred to her. Now that Mike mentioned it, it still made no sense. Tolliver was… had been too arrogant.

"Because he struck me as someone who thought of himself in terms of immortality. Immortals don't kill themselves. They might kill others, but they don't kill themselves." She let the information he'd just passed on sink in. This whole thing was getting weirder by the moment. "I guess then you don't need his permission to take a look at his files now."

The killer had inadvertently made things easier for him. "The drawers to the cabinet were opened, as if someone was looking for something."

"And nobody'd notice a little more 'looking' taking place," Natalya guessed, tongue-in-cheek.

He smiled. God, he'd been thinking of her all

day. She kept popping up in his head, refusing to let him complete an entire thought. "We think alike."

She smiled as he took her into his arms. "I guess we do."

His eyes washed over her, memorizing the subtle features of her face. "So guess what I'm thinking right now."

She raised her eyebrows innocently. "How to solve the square root of pi?"

Mike slowly ran the back of his knuckles against her cheek. "Guess again."

There they went, she thought, all her pulse points going off at once. "You want to skip dinner and go straight to dessert." It wasn't a guess, it was a fact. For both of them.

He laughed, quickly brushing his lips against hers. "We do think alike."

She barely managed to maintain her

innocent expression. "No, I just guessed what *you'd* be thinking, remember?"

"Then you do want to go out to dinner?" Mike deadpanned.

She cocked her head, her smile filtering into her eyes. "Actually, I think that I kind of like your idea about dessert. Just so happens that I had a late lunch today." She didn't add that it was half of Vicki's peanut butter and jelly sandwich. All she could think of was being alone with him.

He paused to kiss her again, this time with more feeling. "Dessert it is."

She could feel the hum of anticipation beginning to throb through her body.

"Kady's got the late shift in the E.R. tonight. We could go to my place." She wanted to make love to him there, in her room. In her bed. "And, to tip the scales," she added, "I actually have food in the refrigerator if you do get hungry."

He leaned his forearms on her shoulders, lacing his hands behind her head. His eyes were intently on hers. "I am hungry," he admitted. "But not for anything that's in your refrigerator."

Her heart crawled up to her throat and lodged itself there.

Okay, she needed to get this out of the way first. The tension of carrying this around was beginning to wear on her. But, she still didn't have a clue how to broach the subject without making it sound as if she was making assumptions about the direction their relationship was heading.

But she had to tell him this before things got any more complicated.

Natalya took a breath, fortifying herself. Praying for inspiration. "Mike, I need to tell you something."

"Okay." Mike's expression was deadly serious. Nerves began to jangle within her. "But first I need to get something out of the way."

But before she could open her mouth to ask what that "something" was, Mike was answering her question by sealing his lips to hers. Within the space of ten seconds, the kneecaps she was trying so hard to save were completely eradicated. Natalya caught herself digging her fingertips into his shoulders to keep from sinking to the floor.

"Now," he murmured, his body heat mingling with hers as he held her close to his chest, "what is it you wanted to say?"

If she told him now, he might not come home with her. And after that preview, all she could think of was being with him. Of making love with him until she was ready to expire from exhaustion.

She shook her head, dismissing the subject. "It'll keep."

"Are you sure?" His eyes searched her face once he'd brushed his lips against hers again.

Was she sure it would keep? No. Was she sure she wanted to make love to him until eternity came to claim her? Absolutely.

"I'm sure," she breathed.

"Good enough for me," he told her.

Not hardly, she responded silently.

The air was heavy with the promise of winter. She could smell it as the wind glided along her face and body despite the warm coat and helmet she had on. The colder it seemed, the more she clung to him, hanging on tightly as much for warmth as any other reason.

They arrived at her apartment building none too soon. She was grateful it wasn't located that far from the hospital or she might have turned into an icicle. Holding on to his shoulders, she dismounted. "I think you need to think about getting a car."

He laughed. He supposed it was cold, but he decided to tease her. "A little brisk air is good for you."

Taking off the helmet, she shook out her hair. It rained like a red river about her shoulders. "What are you planning on doing if it snows?"

"Same thing I did last year when it snowed." He winked. "Wear heavier boots." Mike locked up his helmet and hers, then looked at her as they walked into the building and headed to the elevator. "I thought you liked my motorcycle."

"I do," she said quickly, then turned her face forward so he couldn't read her expression. "I just don't like thinking about you getting sick."

The elevator arrived and they got in. Natalya reached over to the two rows of buttons and pressed for the appropriate floor.

"I never get sick," he told her.

Her fingers nearly didn't make contact with the button. "Never?"

"Never," he answered glibly.

She really doubted that, but she played along. "Does medical science know about you?"

He looked at her significantly, then allowed a smile to slowly unfurl on his lips. "You do."

He made her crazy when he looked at her like that, she thought. She threaded her hand through his. "I think I'll keep you a secret a while longer."

He looked at her in surprise, glancing at her hands. "Your hands *are* cold."

"Next time," she said as they reached her floor and got out, "I'll put them in your pockets."

His eyes were dancing as he walked to her door. "Looking forward to it." He waited until she unlocked the door, then walked in behind her. Once inside, he simultaneously closed the door and pulled her to him. "About that dessert…"

She tilted her head up to his, her eyes on his lips. Warmth spread out through her limbs, coating them. "Coming right up."

It was all the encouragement he needed.

He took his time, making love to every part of her. It had been an extremely long day and he wanted nothing more than to expunge it from his brain.

Wanted, he realized, to think and feel nothing but Natalya until all traces of the day were completely washed away.

Each time he made love with her, it was the same thrill. And yet, it was different.

Mike made love to her in so many ways, she couldn't begin to keep track, couldn't manage to keep up. It was like running beside a train, her belt caught in the door. She couldn't slow down, couldn't catch up. All she could do was run.

He made her aware of all the different, gloriously erotic spots on her body, spots she'd never even known were there. Pleasure mushroomed and spread all through her like liquid sunshine.

She worked hard to please him, to create, at least remotely, the same kind of pleasure for him that he created within her. But it was hard to stay focused on his pleasure when he made her want to do nothing but relish hers.

Each part of her vibrated with anticipation, with desire, with a need to feel and savor what was happening down to the lowest depths of her soul. He made climax after climax erupt through her body like a moment in time forever looped, before finally joining her for the ultimate sensation.

The euphoria that she'd felt growing finally exploded, raining its fragments down around her. Through her.

And then, it withdrew by tiny increments until it was gone. Leaving behind only shadows. And the nagging thoughts that continued to plague her, that whispered along the borders of her mind, reminding her that she was being dishonest by not telling him what he needed to know.

Mike rolled off her and she lay there, staring up at the ceiling, searching for words, at a loss as how to string them coherently together. All she knew was that she loved him and she didn't want this to end. But it would. Once he knew, it would.

"Is this a solitary journey, or can I come along, too?"

It took her a second to realize that he was speaking, another to realize that he'd asked her a question. She turned her face toward him. "What?"

"You look lost in your thoughts," he explained, pulling her closer against his side. "I was just wondering if you were going to let me in on them."

She took a breath, shading her eyes with her hand. With every fiber in her, she tried to block out the sensations his very presence next to her kept resurrecting. "I don't think you really want to know that."

There was something about her tone that made him uneasy, but he pushed on. "Wanting to know is the definition of a detective. Try me."

She almost didn't say it, almost just turned toward him and began to kiss him. But then the words just spilled out. "I can't get pregnant."

Of all the things he would have guessed her saying, this wouldn't have even remotely been on his list. Stunned, Mike sat up and looked at her. "Have you been trying?"

Caught up in her thoughts, his question threw her. "What?"

"I thought you were on birth control pills," he told her, trying to make sense out of what was going on here. "Have you been trying to get pregnant?"

"No!" As if trying would ever make it happen.

"Then—" Words deserted him. He began again. "I don't understand," he confessed, waiting for an explanation.

It hurt even to think about it, much less say it. "I can't get pregnant—ever."

Natalya made it sound like a conscious decision. The thought shook him as he struggled to comprehend. "Because you don't want kids? Because, if it's the profession you're in, don't let it get to you. I've heard a lot of people say that once you have kids of your own, it's different—"

"You're not listening," she insisted, breaking in. "I *can't* have kids. Not because I don't want to but because I physically can't." She felt tears beginning to dampen her eyes and fought them back. She wasn't going to be one of those weak, weepy women. She didn't want him to stay because of tears, but because he loved her. "When I was nineteen, I came down with endometriosis. A really bad case," she emphasized. The mere memory made her want to shiver. "The pain was unbelievable. The doctor cured me so I didn't have to go on enduring a living hell—at least not physically. But…" Her voice trailed off, words deserting her again.

She searched for the best way to put this. But

there was no best way. There was only the painful, barren truth. "The upshot is that I can't have children. That's why I became a pediatrician. I figured that was the only way I'd get to hold a baby in my arms."

Reaching for the robe she kept at the foot of her bed, she turned her back to him as she slipped it on. When she turned around again, he'd gotten dressed.

A knot formed in her stomach.

He's leaving.

She shouldn't have told him. At least, not yet. Not until she had gotten him to the point that he couldn't just walk away from her.

So what had been her plan? To keep him by being silent? That was the sin of omission. And she wasn't the kind of woman to hold on to a man by deception, vocal or silent.

But loving him had made her want to throw

away all the rules, to do anything in her power to make him stay.

If you love something, set it free.

Great words for a philosophy, she thought cynically. Not so great in real life.

The silence threatened to eat her alive. "Say something," she finally implored.

Mike felt as if he'd been kicked in the stomach by a mule.

He was in no hurry for children, but he'd always thought, when he *was* ready, they would come. It was the most natural thing in the world, having children. So many of the people he had been around in the housing projects where he grew up seemed to pop them out every nine months or so. Nothing to it.

And yet, if he made things official with Natalya, if he followed what he felt, there would be no smaller versions of him or her. No sons who wanted to play ball, no daughters to love and protect.

Nothing to it turned into everything to it.

He felt overwhelmed. Not so much betrayed as devastated. And confused. Very confused.

"I need some time to think," was what he finally said.

Natalya wanted to throw herself in front of the door, to talk him out of whatever it was he was thinking. Wanted to change whatever it was that tilted the scales away from her and made him walk out of not just her door, but her life.

A thousand incoherent words flew in and out of her head, but never made it to her tongue. Because she'd only sound like a babbling idiot and she'd rather his last memory of her be not without dignity.

So she said nothing.

And he walked out of her apartment.

Chapter 15

Natalya waited, holding her breath. Willing Mike to come back, to say he'd made a mistake. To say that they could work things out somehow.

Her eyes focused on the door, waiting for a knock, a ring. A voice echoing through the wood.

When first five, then ten minutes had gone by, she knew she was waiting in vain.

Moving like someone caught in a dream set in slow motion, Natalya got dressed again.

With effort, she tried to lose herself in the mechanics of what she was doing and disengage her mind totally.

She couldn't think now, couldn't let herself feel.

One foot in front of the other, that was the best she could hope for right now. Later she could begin a recovery program. If she even attempted it now, she knew she'd fall all to pieces without so much as a prayer of pulling herself together. She had patients who depended on her, a family that loved her. She *couldn't* fall apart. She'd be no good to any of them if she did that.

The emptiness that hovered and grew threatened to overwhelm her. Throwing her shoulders back, Natalya went through the entire apartment, turning on every television set, the main one in the living room and the smaller sets that were in each of the three bedrooms. She needed noise, needed the comfort of the rainbow of lights that flowed from the monitors. Needed to fill the silence, the emptiness.

Moving from room to room, she set each monitor to the same channel and then went to the kitchen to clean counters that were already gleaming and scrub pots that already shone.

Natalya was on her hands and knees, scrubbing the floor, fighting back tears that refused to abate, when she felt it. Felt the press of cold metal against her skin. The slim barrel of a pistol was against the side of her neck.

She hadn't heard him enter, his steps muffled by the noise that surrounded her.

"Where is it?" the deep voice demanded.

Reflexes had her fingers digging into the oversized, soapy sponge she'd been using to clean the floor. But before she could swing around and throw it at the intruder's face, she was being roughly jerked up to her feet.

Her arm felt as if it was being yanked out of its socket. Air whooshed out of her lungs. Natalya found herself looking up into a face obscured by a black ski mask. There were only slits for a mouth and eyes.

Intense, steely, piercing blue eyes that looked as if they could effortlessly vivisect her at a moment's notice.

"Where's what?" she shot back.

Numbed and devastated by Mike's abrupt departure, there was no emotional strength left over for fear. But what she was capable of feeling was anger. There was more than a little beginning to bubble up inside her.

Her retort earned her a backhanded slap across her face that made her stumble backward. The force was so great, there was no telling how far back she would have gone, if there hadn't been a sink at her back. The sudden, abrupt contact was painful. It was like receiving a quick, sharp jab to her kidneys.

Instead of cowering or backing off, Natalya straightened, furious at this invasion. Furious at Clancy's death. And furious at loving a man who apparently couldn't love her back.

"What the hell are you doing here?" she demanded hotly, her very stance challenging the intruder. It was almost as if she didn't even see the gun in his gloved hand.

Rather than answer immediately, the intruder cocked the revolver. When he spoke, his voice was deadly cold. And mocking.

"Look very carefully at the gun, Dr. Pulaski. You're not in any position to do anything but give me what I want."

Inexplicably, she suddenly thought of her underwear drawer. Kady hadn't gone through it, this monster had. She was sorry now that she hadn't attached any weight to that. There *had* been someone in the apartment, looking for something. Not money, because he wouldn't have come back. But then what had he been looking for? What had made him come back a second time?

She had to get him to tell her.

Natalya raised her chin defiantly. "I don't know what you're talking about." Her heart stopped as she saw him raise his gun, aiming the weapon at her head.

It couldn't end here, she insisted silently. It couldn't. She had too much to live for, too much she still had to do.

"Don't play dumb, Doctor," the man snarled. "I'm out of patience and you're out of luck."

Getting hold of himself, he enunciated every word. "Now where is the camera?"

The camera. Clancy's camera.

Natalya felt something sharp skewer her belly. The intruder knew about the camera. Which meant he knew about the photographs.

He was after the photographs.

Suddenly, she looked at the eyes again. Recognition came riding in on a lightning bolt.

"Jessop."

Rage filled his eyes as the intruder swore roundly at the sound of his name. Still pointing the gun at her, he tore off the ski mask with his other hand, exposing his face.

Dark brown hair peaked in unruly tufts as Ralph Jessop stuffed the mask into the pocket of his sheepskin jacket. "No more games," he shouted. "Where the hell is the damn camera?"

He obviously must have found out that Clancy had taken photographs, but from the desperate look on his face, he didn't know that there was nothing in them to implicate him.

Did that buy her a little time, or seal her fate?

She couldn't allow herself to start giving in to fear now.

"With the police." She tossed her head defiantly. Her anger was almost at an unmanaged degree as another realization came to her. Asking for confirmation was just a formality. "Did you kill Clancy?"

He didn't seem to hear the question. What came before it had the whole of his attention. His eyes narrowed into blue lasers. "You're lying. The police don't have the camera."

Was it desperation, or hope, behind his declaration? She had no choice but to brazen it out.

"Why? Because they haven't been by to

arrest you yet? They're busy exhuming bodies so that they can put the final nail in your coffin. They're probably at your office and home right now, armed with a warrant, ready to drag you off to a cell." She could feel her pulse accelerating, moving faster and faster. "If you give yourself up, it'll go easier on you."

"What?" He spat out the word contemptuously. "Life in prison without parole. Sorry, not interested."

He'd given her an answer. Another wave of rage rose up in her throat. She could taste bile. "You *did* kill Clancy."

The doctor didn't seem to see a reason to deny it. The very mention of Clancy darkened the look on his face, making him appear even more malevolent.

"The arrogant son of a bitch had the gall to confront me. Who would have thought someone like him would have had the brains to make the connection?" he scoffed. "Or the morals to care."

The pieces began to come together in Natalya's head. "You couldn't bribe him to keep quiet."

He was less than two feet away from her, the threat of his weapon growing larger by the heartbeat. "I'm not here for a dialogue, Doctor."

He might not be, but she wanted answers. And maybe, if she kept him talking, she could catch him off guard and get the gun away from him. "Why did you do it? You had a good practice, prestige, money—"

He cut her off angrily. Jessop was not a man who put up with being questioned. "Not enough. Not when you owe money to a man with a long reach and no patience." For a split second, Natalya thought she saw weariness, regret, in Jessop's eyes. "No one was supposed to get hurt. Nobody cared about those people and it wasn't as if they were murdered for their organs. They were all already dead. A perfect victimless crime—"

Through the din of background noise, she thought she heard her name being called.

In the next moment, Jessop cut the remaining space between them. He grabbed her, holding the gun barrel to her temple. Cursing, the radiologist jerked her around in front of him, using her as a shield as he turned toward the source of the voice.

"You didn't answer the door," Mike's voice grew closer. "If you didn't have all these damn TVs on—" Reaching the kitchen, he stopped abruptly. His hand went to his weapon.

"Hold it right there," Jessop shouted the warning as if there were yards between them instead of just feet. "One more move and she's dead."

Mike's eyes darted toward Natalya. His expression gave no indication of the fear he felt. "Are you all right?"

Natalya's mouth was bone dry. It had begun to dawn on her that she might not walk away from this.

"I've been better," she allowed, then curved her lips in a quick, spasmodic smile. She didn't want Mike taking any chances on her account. Jessop looked desperate and probably thought he had nothing to lose. Desperate people did terrible things.

"Very touching," Jessop snarled. He waved his weapon at Mike. "Take the gun out of your holster, Detective, and put it on the floor."

"No," Natalya cried, her eyes widening as she looked at Mike. "Don't listen to him." She felt Jessop's grip tighten on her arm. She bit down on her lower lip to keep back any involuntary sound.

"Do as I say," Jessop told him, "or you can watch her die."

She could feel each one of Jessop's fingers digging into her flesh. "Mike, you do and he's going to kill us both."

But Mike slowly shook his head, never taking his eyes off Jessop. "I can't risk it, Natalya."

"You're being very sensible," Jessop jeered. "The gun," he prompted.

Making an elaborate show of taking the weapon out of its holster with his fingertips, Mike cleared it of the leather, then began to bend his knees in order to place the gun on the floor.

Once that was out of his hands, she just knew Jessop was going to shoot. There was nothing in his way and he'd already killed once. Maybe more.

"Mike," Natalya pleaded. Their eyes met for a moment.

The weapon was almost on the floor when Mike shouted her name. She ducked her head a split second before he fired.

The bullet found its target, burrowing into Jessop's forehead right above the bridge of his nose. He jerked backward and fell, his fingers now in a death grip on Natalya's arm. Unable to steady herself, Natalya went down on top of the man who was dead before he hit the floor.

Mike was at her side the same moment, bringing her to her feet. He enfolded her in his arms, holding her close, not saying a word. She felt his heart racing against her own chest.

They stood like that for a long moment before he finally released her just enough to look down at her face. He searched for signs of stress, of fear, and saw none. Hell of a woman, he thought.

Still, he asked, "Are you all right?"

Very slowly, she nodded her head. "He didn't hurt me."

He couldn't wrap his mind around that concept. It held too much fear, too much emotion, for him to deal with. "If he had—"

His voice was trailing off. A hint of gallows humor curved her mouth. "You would have killed him twice?" she asked.

He laughed with relief, with nerves that were yet unspent, and hugged her to him again. Grateful that he could and that she was whole.

"I was going to say I wouldn't have been able to stand it." Mike allowed himself one kiss before he returned to being a detective instead of a man. Stepping back, he squatted over the body to assure himself of what he already knew. Jessop was dead. He spared Natalya a glance. "No confessions coming from him."

She stifled a shiver. "I'd say his being here was confession enough."

There was something in her voice that caught his attention. Mike rose to his feet again. "Did he say anything?"

"Enough to make me think that he was the one running the show." Otherwise, he wouldn't have said what he had about thinking of what he did as victimless crimes. "He killed Clancy."

She said it with such conviction, he didn't think to question her about it. That would come, by and by, when they took her statement at the precinct. For now, it was enough that she was alive and unharmed. "Probably Tolliver, too."

He saw the look on her face. As someone

dedicated to curing people, she undoubtedly had a difficult time understanding how people could willfully destroy life. "But why?"

He gave it his best guess. "He was probably afraid that Tolliver would testify against him in exchange for immunity, or at least a more lenient sentence. First one with his hand up gets the deal." He looked down at the dead man. The mayor is going to want to be briefed, he thought. "We'll investigate this as far as it'll go."

Taking out his cell phone, he put a call into the coroner's office, requesting a van be sent over, along with a forensic team. When he ended the call, he looked up to see Natalya looking at him.

"What?" he wanted to know. Had he overlooked something?

The small smile on her lips widened until it seemed to take over her face. "You came back."

And for that, Mike thought, he would be grateful to his dying day. "Lucky for you," he commented.

She paused for a moment, debating if she was pushing her luck by asking. And then she decided she needed to know. "Don't take this the wrong way, but why did you come back?"

He wasn't given to lying, but neither was he accustomed to wearing his heart on his sleeve. But they had both looked death in the face just now, so he made an exception. "Because I didn't need a week to sort things out."

Each word came out slowly, as if she were holding her breath as she asked. "And what is it that you sorted out?"

His eyes met Natalya's. "That the most important thing about having kids is to give them a loving home with parents who really love each other."

Maybe he didn't understand her before, or maybe he was in denial. As much as she wanted to be with him, as much as she loved him, she couldn't allow any sort of misconceptions to linger. "But Mike, I told you that I can't—"

Mike gently pressed a finger to her lips, stopping the flow of words. He needed her to understand that without her, nothing else mattered.

"I'm not an egotist, Natalya. The children we're going to have don't need to have my blood in their veins to be mine. Besides—" he cleared his throat as he dropped his hand to his side "—we're getting a little ahead of ourselves."

Natalya stiffened. She knew it. He was telling her that she'd leaped to conclusions about their relationship. They might never get to the stage where her being able to have children even mattered. She could feel her cheeks burning as she looked down at the floor. "Right."

"First, I'm going to have to take you home to meet my parents."

Her head shot up. "Excuse me?"

"Was the gunshot too loud?" he asked innocently. Lowering his head, he whispered against her ear. "I want you to meet my parents."

Natalya felt numb all over again. But it was a good numb. She wanted to throw her arms around him, but instead, she deadpanned, "Why?"

"Well, I'm not sure how it goes in your culture, but a good Italian boy always brings the woman he intends to marry home to meet his mother."

She'd thought about it, wanted it, mourned it when she thought it was no longer a possibility. But to hear him actually say it made her almost light-headed. "Marry?"

Amusement echoed in his voice. "That gunshot really did wreak havoc with your hearing, didn't it?"

"But you didn't ask me," she pointed out in her own defense.

"I just did." And then he blew out a breath, feigning resignation. He took her hand in his, then pressed it against his chest. Against his heart. "Natalya Pulaski, I love you and I want you to marry me. It doesn't have to be soon," he added, not wanting to crowd her, "but it does have to be."

Natalya looked at him innocently as the sound of sirens in the distance became audible. "And I have no say in it?"

"Only if it involves the word 'yes.'"

She smiled, lacing her arms around his neck. He slipped his around her waist. "Then lucky for you, that was the word I was thinking."

The sirens grew louder. "Your people are fast. I'd better go and make sure the door's unlocked," she told him, assuming that he'd shut it in his wake when he'd walked in.

She glanced down at the man who had wanted to kill them both. It was over, Clancy was avenged. She felt a weight lifted from her heart.

Mike made no effort to release her.

"Not before I make this official," he told her as she turned her face up to his.

Just before he kissed her.

* * * * *